HOGAN
Hogan, Ray,
Fire Valley :
D0457372

FIRE VALLEY

Fire Valley

A Western Duo

Ray Hogan

FIVE STAR

An imprint of Thomson Gale, a part of The Thomson Corporation

Detroit • New York • San Francisco • New Haven, Conn. • Waterville, Maine • London

Set in 11 pt. Plantin.

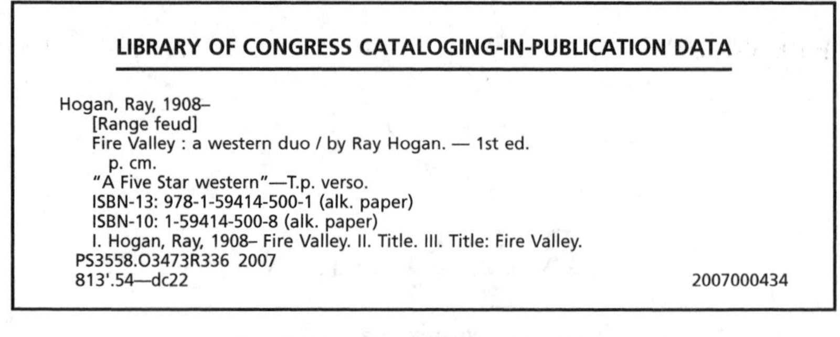

LIBRARY OF CONGRESS CATALOGING-IN-PUBLICATION DATA

Hogan, Ray, 1908–
[Range feud]
Fire Valley : a western duo / by Ray Hogan. — 1st ed.
p. cm.
"A Five Star western"—T.p. verso.
ISBN-13: 978-1-59414-500-1 (alk. paper)
ISBN-10: 1-59414-500-8 (alk. paper)
I. Hogan, Ray, 1908– Fire Valley. II. Title. III. Title: Fire Valley.
PS3558.O3473R336 2007
813'.54—dc22 2007000434

First Edition. First Printing: May 2007.

Published in 2007 in conjunction with Golden West Literary Agency.

Printed in the United States of America on permanent paper
10 9 8 7 6 5 4 3 2 1

CONTENTS

★ ★ ★ ★ ★

Range Feud

★ ★ ★ ★ ★

I

Squatted on his heels, tin of black coffee cupped between his palms, Dan Ragan stared morosely into the dying embers of the fire. Taking a swallow of the hot, bitter liquid, he turned his glance to the east. The predawn gray had faded and now a muddied flare of color was spreading above the ragged horizon. On to the south a long curtain of rain clouds bellied low over the land.

He'd be wet before this day was over, he thought, and wondered about the possibility of there being a town nearby where he could hole up for a spell—at least until the weather cleared. But that was out of the question. There wasn't time to hole up for somewhere close behind him, coming on with the determination of youth and driven by a relentless desire for vengeance, was Jody Strickland. The boy had been on Dan's heels for more than a week now, dogging him from town to town, valley to valley, hill to hill with only one thought in mind—avenge the death of his father.

And it was all a mistake. Oh, Colby Strickland was dead, all right, but there had been good reason for the shooting and it was a fair fight; if there was an edge at all, it had been with the gambler. That had counted for nothing with Jody, however, who had ridden in the day after the shooting had taken place, listened to the account, and made up his own mind. Although he saw little of his father and stepmother, and was aware only that both had known Dan Ragan from the past, he came to conclusions that were far from the facts and decided to ignore the findings of the law and take matters into his own hands. That he was an ordinary cowhand with only average skill with a six-gun while Dan Ragan was numbered among the more deadly meant nothing to him. Common sense was blinded. His entire being was overwhelmed by a fixation on that all too often misinterpreted passage from the Bible—"an eye for an eye"—and such price he vowed to exact from his father's killer, or die trying.

Thus Dan Ragan, a drifter of practice but a man of caliber, wanting no trouble with a boy still two or three years short of legal manhood, had quietly saddled up and moved on. One town was very like another to him and destinations mattered little; he simply wanted it to end there.

Only it hadn't worked out that way. Two nights later he encountered Jody Strickland in the Lone Pine Saloon at Vegas. He had been surprised to see the boy—and considerably disturbed to learn that Jody had not abandoned his threat but fully intended to make good each and every word uttered. Jody Strickland had trailed him, and would continue to do so until there was a showdown and the score was settled; Dan realized that for the first time as he studied the boy's intent, hating face that night in the smoky, odorous depths of the saloon.

A commotion at the far end of the room had provided a distraction and Ragan, taking advantage of it, had slipped out a side door, mounted hurriedly, and ridden on. The irony of the situation had touched him that night—he, who had never run from any man, who met trouble when and where it came on whatever basis necessary, was fleeing before a mere boy. Why? Ragan found difficulty in answering the question. That he could gun down Jody with ease was a foregone conclusion, that he would be well within his rights to stop and, challenged, protect himself was also true. But he found himself unwilling to handle the problem in this manner. He would keep moving, elude Jody, and avoid a confrontation in which he would be forced to kill the boy or allow himself to die. It wasn't too great a price to pay—at least he didn't think so at first.

But Dan Ragan's patience was wearing a little thin. He'd hoped and expected to throw Jody off his trail within the first few days, had even entertained the idea that the boy would weary of the chase and turn back. Neither had proved to be the case. Jody was still there, patiently following his trail, a day or two at most behind.

Glum, Ragan looked again to the south. Mexico lay there, on beyond that mist of low mountains. The Sierra Madres might offer good opportunity for shaking the boy. Or he could cut east across Texas, make his way to New Orleans, board a steamer, and double back up the Mississippi to some point where he could disembark and head west again into home country. Doubtless such would throw Jody off—but would it end there? There was no reason to believe so; the look in the boy's eyes that night in the Lone Pine made it plain he was prepared to spend the remainder of his life in the pursuit of vengeance, if necessary.

Ragan shrugged, tossed the last of the coffee into the now dead fire, and got to his feet. It was a problem he couldn't solve except in the one obvious way—and he was still unwilling to accept that. For the time being he'd just continue to dodge Jody. Perhaps something would develop, a means for handling the situation without resorting to gun play.

For a long minute he stood at the edge of the clearing, high up on a slope overlooking a valley—the Lagrima Valley he'd heard it was called—and let his gaze run over the softly contoured land. A tall, lean man with gray eyes that appeared almost white at times in the deep-set pockets of his dark face, there was a quiet patience to him; it was as if time and experience had tutored him well, instilled in him the belief that all things worked out in the end—that all tribulations passed and became a part of the past, finally.

Again he shrugged and, turning, ambled slowly in the manner of a man unaccustomed to doing much walking, toward the edge of the clearing where he had staked his horse. Leading the bay back into camp proper, he threw his gear into place and proceeded to get the big horse ready for the day's traveling. He did it methodically, carefully, and with the deft, sure motions of a man who had accomplished the chore countless times without conscious thought.

Finished, he picked up the small lard tin that he carried for coffee brewing, dumped the grounds and remaining few drops of liquid into the fire. Then, nesting the dented cup inside the tin, he thrust it into the right-hand pocket of his saddlebags, pulled tight the buckles. Taking a final look around to assure himself that he was forgetting nothing, he stepped into the stirrup and swung onto his well-worn hull.

"Time to move on, horse," he muttered to the bay. "You get yourself a hunch how we can lose that boy, I'll be much obliged."

The bay simply waited and then, at the lift of the reins, came about and moved slowly toward the faint trail that crossed the south edge of the clearing.

The quick slap of gunshots, coming from the valley below, brought Ragan to abrupt attention. He drew in the gelding, cocked his head to one side as he endeavored to pinpoint the location of the sound. It seemed to come from directly beneath him, and he wondered if there was a ranch there on the floor of the valley—or perhaps it was a road and a hold-up, of a stagecoach likely, was in progress.

More shots broke out—a dozen or more in quick succession, indicating that several guns were involved. Frowning, Ragan touched the bay with his spurs. He'd best have a look.

II

The first thing to catch Ragan's attention as he looked down the long slope was the dull, silver gleam of a small river winding its way through a carpet of lush grass and stalwart trees. It was apparent that he was somewhere near center of the vast valley as he could see, despite the early morning haze, that the broad cleavage extended for miles to both the north and south. The bay, mincing cautiously, moved nearer to a break in the rim of the butte, halted. Ragan saw the ranch then—a scatter of small, unimpressive buildings and corrals placed not far from the foot of the hillside. Half a dozen riders were whipping back and forth across the yard between what was evidently the main house and the barn.

They were shooting their pistols indiscriminately. A horse lay dead near a hitch rack at the side of the house. Close to the rear door a dog had met a similar fate. Dust was spurting from walls, from hoofs, from the rails of the corrals as bullets dug into their surface.

Dan Ragan, frowning, studied the scene thoughtfully. Except for the raiders, the ranch appeared to be deserted. He could see no one moving inside the house, and there were no answering gunshots coming from any of the buildings. That could only mean the attack was being made while the owner was absent.

The conclusion had scarcely cleared Dan's mind when a hunched figure spurted from the doorway of the barn, started across the hard pack for the main house at a dead run. One of the raiders spotted the man, hauled up short, wheeled. His arm came up slowly, deliberately. The pistol in his hand bucked; smoke coiled from the weapon. The running man paused in mid-stride. His legs seemed to freeze, half bent, and then suddenly he was rolling in the dust.

At once two more figures broke from the shelter of the barn—a young woman and a boy. Heedless of the yelling, shooting riders, they rushed toward the fallen man. The raiders wheeled into a tight knot at the far end of the yard, came about. Immediately they began to lay down a barrage of bullets, placing a barrier between the wounded man and the pair who hurried to aid him.

The stricken man stirred, raised himself partly, and waved them back. Both hesitated. Then, as a fresh burst of gunshots sent dust spurting over their feet, the boy seized the woman's hand and, after a moment's insistence, persuaded her to hurry back to the safety of the barn with him.

Ragan shifted uneasily on the saddle. Three people having trouble with raiders—with the odds all against them. Apparently they had been caught away from the house unarmed, were unable to fight back. The older man had made an effort to reach the house, get his hands on a weapon—had gotten himself shot down. The young woman and the boy had tried to help, were driven off. What was it all about? There could be a dozen or more answers to the question, Ragan knew—a local feud, bad blood between adjacent ranchers, an unsettled range problem, a killing. None of it was his business and he had no call to horn in.

He had to keep moving on, anyway. Jody Strickland was not far away. If he paused to lend a hand—butt in on somebody else's affairs, actually—he'd be setting himself up for the one thing he was trying to avoid, a showdown with the boy. Ride on!

Ragan lifted the bay's reins, brought him about, and pointed him toward the trail at the edge of the flat that would take him on to the south—to Mexico. A new splatter of gunshots halted him, drew his attention to the swale below.

The girl—alone—was trying to reach the man sprawled in the dust. Near the house two of the raiders were dragging up dry brush, piling it against the walls while a third was building himself a torch of dry twigs. The remaining horsemen were sweeping down on the girl. Dan could hear them yelling, laughing. One, a squat-looking dark man, leaned well over in his saddle, arm crooked and ready to catch her up as he swooped by, to carry her off. As he bore in, she dodged frantically to one side. The rider missed and, as his horse swerved sharply, lost balance and tumbled to the ground.

He was up instantly to the cheers and laughter of his companions. He brushed at his mouth, shoved his hat to the back of his head, and hunched forward, started for the girl. She halted, drew up stiffly. Abruptly she abandoned her hopes of reaching the wounded man and began to head back to the barn. The rider said something to her. She wheeled, began to run—stumbled.

The girl was up instantly, but the delay had been long enough to turn the advantage to the raider. He was upon her in the next moment. One hand shot out, grasped her wrist, the other clawed into her hair. With a heave he threw her off balance to the ground. Bending swiftly, he pinned her flat with a knee while he maintained his hold upon her arm and the thick folds of her dark hair. Raising his head, he looked at his grinning friends.

"Come on, you yahoos! We're going to have us some fun!"

In that next instant all Dan Ragan's strict rules against meddling in other's problems were forgotten—along with his recently resolved determination to keep out of Jody Strickland's way. Jerking out his pistol, he spun the bay around and, roweling the big horse sharply, sent him through the break of the butte's rim and plunging recklessly down the steep grade.

The thunder of the bay's hoofs, the racket of spilling gravel and crackling brush, drew immediate attention. One of the raiders lifted his gun, fired. The bullet splatted against a ledge just below Dan Ragan.

Instantly he snapped a return shot. The man drew off,

wheeled away. Dan threw another, more carefully aimed bullet at the raider crouched over the girl. The man's angry face was turned to him. The slug went true. The raider jolted, staggered to his feet, yelling. Clutching his shoulder, he headed for his waiting horse.

Ragan, drawing near the foot of the slope, aimed another shot at the three men endeavoring to start a fire against the north wall of the house. They had paused at the sound of his approach and now, with one of their party wounded, seemed to be in doubt as to whether to continue their activities relative to arson—or run.

Finally on the level at the bottom of the grade, Ragan sent the bay charging forward with another rake of the spurs. Crooking his left arm, he rested his pistol upon it, pressed off a shot at the man nearest the house. The rider sagged, began to fall from the saddle, caught himself. Clawing at the reins, he got his horse cut around and, at a rough trot, pointed for a grove of trees a quarter mile distant.

The others continued to mill about, attempting to get a clean shot at Ragan. But he was cutting back and forth, dodging in behind the smaller sheds, out again, offering no target. Two of their number had been hit while he had gone untouched despite the half dozen guns turned against him, and he was still coming on. That knowledge was having its disturbing effect upon them.

Ragan drew abreast the girl, now kneeling beside the wounded man. He looked down into her strained features.

"Get him inside!" he yelled. "I'll hold them off long as I can!"

White-lipped, the girl nodded, cast a glance to the barn where the boy had reappeared and was running to join her.

Ragan swept on by. His pistol was almost empty, he realized grimly, and time for reloading was going to be hard to come by. He swung his attention to the brush off to the right, noting suddenly that the raiders had come together in a close knot at the end of the house. He had them all before him in a single group. Discarding the thought of veering off and reloading, he leaned forward, pressed off his last bullet, sending it directly into the midst of the raiders.

A yell of pain went up. Abruptly they broke apart, wheeled, and at a hard gallop rode for the grove into which their injured partner had disappeared.

III

Ragan immediately curved in behind a small shed, using his knees to guide the bay while he punched the empties from his pistol and pressed fresh cartridges into the cylinder from the supply in his belt. He glanced over his shoulder, saw the girl and the young boy moving toward the house, supporting the wounded man between them. He was badly hit, Dan knew as he swung his horse around and headed into the open yard where he could see the grove. There was a slack, gray look to the fellow's face and the upper part of his linsey shirt was soaked with blood.

Halting in the center of the hard pack, Ragan turned his attention to the distant trees. He could barely distinguish one rider just within the brush that fringed the grove. The others were there, however, he was certain of that. They would be doctoring up their wounded, deciding what next should be done. It was a bit different now; no longer were the owners of the ranch trapped in the barn, unable to fight back. They now had access to weapons.

Dan Ragan shrugged. A young woman and a boy—and a man who probably wouldn't last out the day. They'd not be able to put up much of a fight even if. . . .

"Mister."

At the hesitant summons, Dan came about on the saddle.

The girl was standing on the porch, her face taut as she looked at him. She was a bit older than he'd figured; around twenty, he supposed. Had dark hair and blue eyes.

"Can . . . can you help us . . . please? My brother is in a bad way."

Ragan did not move. His jaw set solidly as a small warning bell somewhere back in his mind began to ring. He'd already horned in more than he should; if he knew what was good for him, wanted to play it smart, he'd make up some excuse, ride on after telling the girl he'd send help.

"Please. I'm new here . . . from the city. I don't know what to do."

Ragan again looked to the grove. The raiders were still there, still well concealed in the thick growth. He guessed it wouldn't hurt to have a look at the wounded man—her brother, she'd said. Swinging the bay around to the hitch rack, he dismounted, flipped the leathers around the bar, and stepped up onto the narrow porch. The girl met him with a relieved smile and crossed to the door.

"This way."

He followed her through the kitchen, down a short hall, and into a small bedroom. The injured man, his eyes dull, mouth slack, lay upon the bed placed beneath the one window where a clean, starched curtain stirred lightly in the breeze. The boy—no more than fifteen, if that, Ragan guessed—stood nearby. Dan centered his attention on him.

"That bunch hasn't pulled out yet. Still hanging around in that grove of trees. Don't know what they're apt to do next. Want you to keep an eye on them while I'm in here . . . let me know quick if they head back this way."

The boy glanced uncertainly at the girl. She nodded, said: "Go ahead, Earl."

He hurried away, and Ragan sat down on the edge of the

bed, began to pull aside the bloody folds of shirt plastered to the man's chest. At the attention, he stirred. His eyes opened a bit wider and a tired smile came to his lips.

"Obliged. My name's Buckman. Pogue Buckman. That's my sister, Ann. Young fellow's my brother Earl. You got here just in time, Mister . . . ?"

"Dan Ragan."

"Mister Ragan . . . appreciate your help. Reckon our numbers would've been up if you hadn't stopped."

Dan laid the last of the shirt aside, studied the wound. The bullet hole was a neat puckered spot, draining steadily. It didn't look too bad from the outside, but Ragan knew that it all depended upon the damage the bullet had done within the man's body. He glanced at the girl.

"Can use some clean rags for bandages. Be needing hot water, too. Try to fix him up until we can get a doctor."

"There's not one . . . not closer than a day's ride, anyway," Ann murmured in a hopeless voice and turned for the door.

Pogue Buckman, eyes fastened upon Dan's browned features, again forced a smile. "Didn't want her touching me. Know what I'm up against. If the doc lived next door, he couldn't do anything for me. Filling up inside."

Dan nodded. "Was afraid that was it. Bullet nicked an artery. Wish there was something I could do."

Pogue Buckman managed to nod. "There is. Just act like everything'll turn out all right. Put on the bandages, make it look good."

Ragan said: "Sure, but your sister and your brother, they ought to know. . . ."

"Not right away. Like to keep it from them long as I can. Reckon I can last till dark."

"Probably. No way of telling."

"Got a little time, anyway . . . and a little's all I'll need.

Enough to talk over a few things, if you'll sort of stick around."

Dan got slowly to his feet. "Not meaning to be blunt and unfeeling, but the fact is I've got to keep moving right along. Little problem of my own. Soon as I get you fixed up, best I ride out. . . ."

His words broke off as Ann reëntered the room, bringing with her a kettle of steaming water, a shallow, tin wash basin, and several folds of clean, white cloth. She placed it all on the table beside the bed and sat down next to her brother. Pouring out a small quantity of the hot water, she folded a strip of cloth into a pad, soaked it, and began to dab at the crusted blood around the wound. She went at the task gingerly, almost fearfully.

"Guess you'd best let me handle that," Dan said, moving her aside gently.

She gave way willingly, and, after she had stepped back out of the way, Ragan set to work dressing the wound properly. He could only hope to slow down the bleeding with compress bandages, but these he realized were simply measures designed to humor the dying man and keep the inevitable fact of death from his sister and young brother. Finally finished, he moved away from the bed. Buckman gave him a worn smile.

"Obliged," he murmured. He was a wide-faced, sandy-haired man with the scars of hard work showing plainly on him. But that was all softening now, just as his coloring was turning to muddy gray as the end drew nearer.

"Isn't there anything else we can do?" the girl asked anxiously, again moving to her brother's side. "He looks so . . . so pale . . . empty."

Pogue reached for her hand, took it in his. "It's all been done. Nothing more left. Mister Ragan'll send the doctor back when he gets to town."

Ann whirled to Ragan, eyes bright with worry. "You can't

stay? I was hoping you'd help . . . not leave. With my brother so bad. . . ."

"How can he send back the doctor and stay, too?" Pogue Buckman chided. "Besides, he has important business of his own to tend."

Ann stirred wearily. "Of course. I wasn't thinking." After a moment she added: "Is there anything I should be doing for him until the doctor arrives?"

Dan looked away, unwilling to meet the girl's pleading eyes. "Nothing much. Keep him warm. Little soup of some kind would help."

"Chicken broth. I can make it right away."

"Be fine. Help to keep up his strength."

Ann turned toward the door, a frown still puckering her brow. She stepped out into the hallway, paused, seemed about to ask something. She was not being fooled much, Dan guessed, and was on the brink of putting the question to him bluntly. At once he swung about, placed his back to her, hoping to block the possibility. He stood that way for a long minute, and then shortly he heard her moving about in the kitchen. He glanced at Pogue, grunted in relief.

"Not going to keep this from her for long," he said quietly.

Buckman's head moved slightly in agreement. "What I'm thinking. Need to tell her. Earl, too. But I'm afraid. . . ."

"Your sister's a grown woman. Boy's no baby. They'll face up to it."

"Reckon I know that. But they're new to this kind of life, this country. Always lived in a city back East. Hard for them to accept things like this. Top of that, me being older, always was me looking out for them, doing their thinking. . . ."

Ragan rubbed at his chin. Pogue Buckman should have known the day would come when his sister and brother would have to face the world on their own. Handling it the way he had, assuming all the responsibilities, would now make it doubly hard for them. But he made no comment; it was Buckman's problem.

Pogue shifted weakly. He was growing worse steadily. A drink of whiskey would be of help, something to quicken his pulse. Dan mentioned the fact to the wounded man. Buckman pointed to a wardrobe standing in the corner of the room.

"Bottle in there. Never was much of a hand to drink."

Dan crossed to the closet, located the almost full quart of rye. Returning to the bed, he uncorked the bottle, handed it to Pogue.

"Take a shot sort of regular. It'll keep you going, same as that soup your sister's making will help. Between the two you might fool us all . . . make it until we can get the doc here."

Buckman took a long pull at the liquor, swallowed with effort, settled back. He lay quietly for a long minute, and then a bit of color seemed to creep into his face and a small smile pulled at his lips. Once more he raised the bottle to his mouth.

"Does help," he murmured, and drank again. Satisfied, he set the liquor on the table beside the bed. "We'll leave it right there, where it'll be handy."

Ragan said nothing, simply moved his head slightly. He should be mounting up, riding on—if that's what he intended to do. The raiders had apparently backed off, weren't making another try—and Jody Strickland was still coming on.

"Beginning to think now that it don't matter much," Pogue said, his voice showing strength. "I mean holding out until sundown, or maybe longer. Ain't nothing I can change."

"Maybe not, but from what I've seen . . . and what you've told me . . . I think you'd better do some talking to your sister and kid brother, sort of get them set for what's going on around here." Ragan paused, jerked his head in the general direction of the grove. "Just what the hell is going on, and who are those gun-happy jaspers out there?"

Pogue Buckman stirred. His eyes were less dull and the lines around his mouth had tightened. "Some of Ross Chandler's hired hands. He's a big rancher in these parts. Owns the spread below and the one above me. Been trying to get me to. . . ."

There was the sound of running in the hall. Buckman's words broke off. Dan turned to the door. Earl, face pale, burst into the room.

"Those men . . . they're coming this way!"

IV

Cursing at the fates under his breath, Dan Ragan wheeled for the door, halted as Ann, carrying a tray upon which were a bowl of broth, a spoon, and several slices of bread, appeared in the opening. He stepped aside, allowing her to enter. But she saw the grimness in his eyes, paused.

"What . . . ?"

"Stay in here," he snapped in an angry, frustrated voice. "You, too," he added, touching the boy with his glance. "Don't want either of you showing yourself."

Hurrying down the hallway, he crossed the kitchen to the doorway, stepped out onto the porch. He could hear the *thud* of the approaching horses but they were still hidden from him by the corner of the house.

Stepping off the landing, he trotted to a small shed standing midway to the barn and drew in behind it. Dropping to a crouch, he peered around the edge at the yard. A grunt of satisfaction slipped from his lips. From that position he had an open view of the house and all the area surrounding it—except, of course, for the opposite front side.

A few moments later the riders appeared. There were only two: a thin-faced man wearing a brown hat with a torn brim, and a somewhat younger cowpuncher with a striped vest. Both were walking their mounts while they swung their heads back and forth from side to side, searching the yard, the house, and all other places for possible danger.

Ragan studied them coldly. There should be two or perhaps even three more in the gang. He'd trimmed the odds some, he knew, but not to the point where only two men remained. It could only mean the bunch had split up, were working in from different points.

He flung a glance to his right. It was a dozen yards to a line of thin brush. To the left lay the yard and a lengthy stretch of open ground before the barn could be reached. Directly behind him, a few strides away, was the first of the corrals. The posts appeared strong and were linked with two-inch-thick planks.

Instantly he wheeled, raced to the pen. Not intending to get inside, he hunkered along the lower timbers, once more putting his attention on the yard. He felt better where he was. At least he had protection to his back.

The two riders had not seen him drop back, the shed standing in between them and the corral and thus blocking his movements. He kept his eyes fastened on the area beyond the small structure and then, shortly, he saw them appear. Both were glancing nervously toward the main house, taking care to remain well back and offer no target to anyone who might be waiting in the rear of the structure.

The faint, dry *snap* of a branch off in the undergrowth to Ragan's right brought him around swiftly. A man, hunched low over his saddle, was moving slowly through the tall weeds and brush. He gained the edge of the growth, halted. A moment later he whistled softly to the pair near the shed. Both lifted their hands in recognition. The cowpuncher, a narrow-faced, hawk-nosed man, settled back to wait.

A second whistle came from across the yard—from beyond a pile of firewood dragged in for winter's use. Again the mounted men gave their acknowledging signal.

It was clear to Dan what was taking place. The raiders thought he and the Buckmans were all inside the main house, that they were trapped once again. He grinned. Unless there were others moving in from behind the barn, which was doubtful, all of the raiders were in front of him—under his gunsight.

"You in the house!" It was the cowpuncher with the torn hat. "Come out with your hands up!"

Ann and Earl Buckman would follow his order, ignore the shout he was sure. And Pogue certainly was in no condition to comply even if he wanted to. There was something else. Evidently there were but four raiders left in the party; otherwise the man doing the talking would have waited for others to get into position.

"You hear me, Buckman? This here's Dave Yates talking. You know me . . . I ain't fooling around none. And we know you're shot up plenty. I'm giving you all a chance to get out before we burn the place down, like we started to do."

Ragan edged forward slightly. He had a good, open view of Yates and the man with him in the center of the yard as well as the rider to his right. The cowpuncher near the woodpile was not so visible, however; he could duck back at the break of trouble, be out of the line of fire.

There was little he could do about it except attempt to drive the man away from his shelter with a few quick bullets if and when it came down to that, Dan decided, and swung his attention back to the men in the yard.

The one in the striped vest was putting a torch together again.

"You hear, Buckman?" Yates repeated. "Come on out while you've got a chance . . . the whole bunch of you. Denver's just about got hisself a torch made. There ain't much time left."

"That's for sure!" the man with him declared. "One way or another we're burning down this here shanty. You want to stay inside, be all right with us."

"Last call!" Yates shouted. "Ain't no sense in. . . ."

Ragan, pistol in hand, one eye cocked toward the man near the woodpile, stepped away from the corral.

"You're not burning anything down!" he called in a strong voice, and then, as sudden motion to his right caught the tail of his eye, he dipped, snapped a shot at the rider hiding in the brush.

The man swore harshly in pain, went to one knee. Dan, spinning fast, changed position, the thought flashing through his mind that he'd guessed wrong; he'd expected trouble from the left—from the man partly hidden by the woodpile. It had come instead from the opposite side of the yard.

"Now I'll be giving some orders!" he continued. "Want all of you with your hands up where I can see them easy. Stand pat, unless maybe you'd like a bullet where it won't do you much good, like your partner there in the weeds."

The two men on their horses in the yard near the shed had come around. The one called Denver dropped the torch he was holding, lifted his arms. Yates followed suit more reluctantly. The raider near the woodpile, evidently fearing the possibility of other defenders hiding elsewhere around the buildings, dropped his pistol, and with hands raised stepped into the open.

Yates, his eyes burning, stared at Ragan. "Who the hell are you, cowboy? You another Buckman?"

Dan shrugged. "Can't see as it makes a difference."

The wounded man in the brush groaned loudly. He was sitting on the ground, both hands clapped to the wound in his thigh. Yates considered him briefly, came back to Dan. "You sure you know what you're buying into, siding in with these jacklegs?"

He was groping in the dark, Ragan realized, not sure of anything. All he knew was that these men of Chandler's were here to wipe out the Buckmans, once and for all time. Maybe Chandler had good reason; maybe the Buckmans deserved it. And he was lining up on the wrong side in the argument. It wasn't always the big rancher who was at fault. He guessed it really didn't matter. He was a sucker for pitching in with the underdog, helping out folks who got caught on the short end of the stick. Anyway, soon as he got things sort of quieted down, he'd be moving on.

"Something else that don't make any difference. What does is that you're trespassing on Buckman land. Telling you now, this better be the last time."

Denver came up stiffly on his saddle. "Who the hell you think you are telling us . . . ?"

"I'm the one holding a bead on your heart with a Forty-Five," Ragan cut in coldly. "Smart thing you can all do is ride out before anybody else gets hurt. Not so good at keeping score, but I figure you've got three men shot up . . . another 'n' nicked. No point making it worse."

"Your brother, Pogue," Yates said. "He's got a slug or two in him. Don't be forgetting that."

They were convinced he was a relative. Ragan let it go without making any correction. Perhaps it might serve to help Ann and the boy, Earl, when he was gone.

"I'm not. And you'd better start praying he gets over it," Dan said, and then jerked his head at the wounded rider. "One of you get over here and give your brush-jumping friend a hand . . . then pull out. Don't think there's any need for more jawing."

Yates bobbed his head at Denver. "Go ahead, Steve. Can't leave him, that's for sure."

Denver crossed the yard to the brush line, halted, and dismounted. Sliding his arm under the wounded man's shoulders, he helped him onto his horse, and then swung back onto his own mount. Side-by-side they returned to Yates. The man near the woodpile had not moved, stood waiting, his eyes on Ragan, seemingly awaiting permission.

Dan gave him a brisk nod. "You're included."

At once the cowpuncher took a step back, grasped the reins of his horse, and mounted. The four men collected in the center of the yard, faces sullen. Dan moved in nearer, arms crossed over his chest, pistol cocked and ready in his right hand.

"Reckon you know this ain't ending here," Yates said in a low voice.

Ragan shrugged. "Up to you . . . and that boss of yours, Chandler, or whatever his name is. It'd be smart."

"Smart thing'd be for you to get your snout out of something that ain't none of your butt-in," Steve Denver snapped.

"Only maybe it is my butt-in," Ragan said softly. "Now, move off . . . and let's don't have any heroes. I'll put a bullet in the first man that even acts like he wants to look back. That clear?"

Yates glared for a long moment, and then abruptly spurred about and headed out of the yard, followed closely by the others.

V

Dan Ragan walked slowly toward the house, never once taking his eyes off the departing riders. They'd be back, just as promised—and next time they would come in a larger force and it would all end up differently.

He reckoned it shouldn't worry him any. He had to push on for Mexico, take care of his own problems—just as Ann and Earl Buckman should face theirs. They should go to the local lawman, enlist his aid. It was a tough break, Pogue Buckman's taking a fatal bullet as he had, but that was the way things worked out sometimes. At any rate they shouldn't expect him to step into their older brother's boots and take over. Ann and the boy would just have to return to that city in the East, pick up the life they had left there. He doubted they were cut out to be ranchers, anyhow. And the way things seemed to be in Lagrima Valley, they'd sure not live long enough to learn. Best course they could follow, when it was all over with Pogue, would be to pull stakes. That's what he was learning to do—move on. Jody Strickland was seeing to that.

He halted at the corner of the main house. The raiders were small shapes now to the north and riding steadily. Wheeling, Ragan backtracked to the porch and, stepping up, crossed and entered the kitchen. Earl was waiting just inside for him, a tight but glowing look on his face.

"You sure got rid of them . . . ," he began in a proud voice.

"They'll be back," Ragan cut in bluntly. "How's your brother?"

The boy was crestfallen. "Better, I guess. Was the soup that helped. Or maybe the liquor."

Dan nodded and walked the short hallway to the bedroom. Ann had raised the oilcloth window shade to the top and the quarters were more cheerful. Pogue did appear to be better with a new strength showing in his eyes, but it could be only a temporary improvement brought about, as Earl had said, by food and drink. Nodding slightly to Ann, he moved to the bed, grinned down at the rancher.

"Keep this up and you'll be on your feet before the day's gone."

Pogue Buckman returned the smile. "Like to believe that." He motioned toward the yard. "Expect that was the first time ever that somebody buffaloed Ross Chandler's bunch. Sure don't know how to thank you."

"No need," Ragan murmured. "Question is . . . what are you aiming to do now? Thing's not over."

"Know that. Was wondering about you . . . talking to Ann about it. I've got a little cash, not much, but some. Like to hire you, your gun. . . ."

Ragan shook his head. "No, thanks. Not that I don't hire out sometimes, all depending on what the trouble is, but truth is I've got to keep riding. Headed for Mexico."

A look of concern flashed across Ann's face. She whirled to him impulsively. "Please, won't you reconsider? I . . . we were hoping you'd stay on, help us. With my brother hurt, helpless. . . ."

"Real important that I keep going," Ragan said.

"But if you go," Earl said from the doorway, "what'll we do? Those men are coming back. Told me that yourself. And with Pogue hurt, they'll just. . . ."

The boy's words trailed hopelessly off into silence. Dan shifted impatiently. "What's this all about? Why are they so set on wiping you out?"

Pogue Buckman reached for the bottle of whiskey, took a long drink. Setting the container back on the table, he brushed shakily at his mouth, turned slightly to face Dan better.

"That bunch you ran off, they all work for Chandler. One doing most of the talking was Dave Yates, sort of a hatchet man for him. One with Dave was Steve Denver. They sort of go together. Never got a look at the others, but they're all a hard bunch. About the only kind Ross Chandler hires nowadays."

"Chandler's the big noise around here, I take it."

"Man at the bottom of all the trouble in Lagrima Valley. Big rancher and wanting to get even bigger. When I took over my place, six years ago, Ross had the ranch north of me. Big place. Over a hundred thousand acres counting the open range he just claimed."

Buckman paused, lay quietly for several moments, breathing heavily. Ann moved toward the bed. He waved her back and again reached for the whiskey, took a swallow. His lips were colorless, Dan noted, and the skin of his face was taking on a slackness once more.

"Was all right with me, of course. Had all the ground I needed, so I didn't pay no mind to what he was doing. Then one day I woke up to find he'd bought out the folks below me, to the south, and I was setting right in the middle between his two big spreads."

Dan stirred. "Not hard to figure what came next. He began wanting your place since it split his range into two pieces."

Pogue nodded. "Exactly the way it was. Came to me, offered to buy me out. Told him I wasn't interested. He tried a couple more times, then, when he saw that I meant it, he started getting mean and trying to force me."

Again Buckman paused, weariness dragging at him. Ann stepped up to the bed, laid a hand upon his forehead.

"You shouldn't talk. It's taking your strength."

The wounded man studied the girl's features thoughtfully, apparently wondering if he should confide in her, should mention the fact that within a few more hours he'd have no need for strength—or anything else. He decided against it.

"Doing fine," he murmured, lips drawing back again into a forced smile. "And it's something I figure Ragan ought to know."

Ann shrugged indifferently. "Why? He's already said he must ride on, that he can't take time to help us because he's busy."

"Not exactly the way of it," Ragan said, touching her with a cool glance. "Got a man snapping at my heels, hoping to catch up and kill me. Just aiming to stay out of his reach."

A shocked expression claimed Ann's face. Pogue frowned, and Earl, his amazement and disbelief evident, darted impulsively into the room.

"You running from somebody!" he exclaimed. "I ain't going to believe that! I'll bet you ain't scared of . . . !"

"Not a case of being scared. If we ever came together, I'd probably drop him before he could clear leather."

Ann stared at him. "Then why . . . ?"

Ragan shrugged off the question. "Personal business. Just put it down that I don't want the time to come when I'll have to face him."

Earl started to protest, say more. Pogue caught his eye. "Let it go, boy," he said. "If Ragan wanted us to know about it, he'd speak out."

Silence dropped over the small room, a stillness broken only by the raspy sound of Buckman's labored breathing and the busy chirping of sparrows outside the window in the vines that covered the side of the house. Finally Pogue began to speak, now in a sort of wandering, reminiscent way.

"Lost quite a few head of cattle. Some'd been shot. Some poisoned. Once they stampeded a bunch over a bluff. Was a terrible thing. Fall didn't kill some of them, just busted them up. Had to take my rifle, end their suffering."

"You saying Chandler did all that?"

"Who else? Never could prove it . . . any of it. But just the same, everybody knew who done it."

"You go to the law?" Ragan asked.

"Something we don't have around here. Not close, anyway. Hard day's ride to Mason City. That's where the sheriff is."

"No town closer than that?"

"Sure. Rock Crossing, if you want to call a saloon and a general store a town. Down the valley about twenty miles, on the river. No marshal or deputy or anything like that there. Here in the Lagrima country man just sort of looks out for himself."

"Still ought to bring that sheriff at Mason City in on your trouble. You've got a right to protection."

"Did talk to him about it once. Right after I come across a bunch of fifty or so steers that'd been shot . . . slaughtered while they were bedding down. Couldn't prove anything, but I told him . . . name's McGaffey . . . I was dead sure it was Chandler's doings. He sort of agreed, I think, and he told me quick he had nothing to go on, but he did ride over and have a talk with Chandler. Didn't accuse him, I heard, just sort of let him know he had suspicions and that he'd better watch his step."

"It help any?"

"Some. Things sort of quieted down after that. I got to thinking Chandler had given up and was going to forget about my land. Was no need for it anyway. Strip of ground fronting my property was four miles wide and open range. No trouble for him to cross back and forth any time he wanted. So I began to feel better about it. Figured the trouble was settled, in fact. All this time Ann and Earl had been waiting back home, getting by, doing the best they could until I got things up to where I had a place for them. Were having it tough, I knew, so when it looked like I'd have no more problems with Chandler, I sent for them. Was a little over a month ago. Now, I'm wishing I'd waited a bit longer."

"No need to be sorry," Ann said. "You couldn't have known things would change."

"Ought've been sure, though. Now, here we are, all boxed in, me hurt and no way to get help. Hired hands have all been run off. And I doubt if there's two dozen steers left alive on the place. . . ."

Dan Ragan turned, crossed slowly to the window, and looked out over the land. He could see the slightly rolling hills to the south from there, little else.

"This is the first time he'd made trouble for you since the sheriff warned him?"

"Second," Pogue replied, his voice beginning to lag. "Him and a gunslinger who works for him . . . Jim Korello . . . came by a week or so ago. Told me flat out I'd better take his offer to buy or get set for all hell . . . to break loose. I . . . I ordered him off the place. Told him to stay off. Then Korello pulled his pistol and started shooting up the ground around my feet. I didn't do no dancing, so he then started shooting things around the yard . . . the wash tub Ann uses . . . couple . . . of the . . . chickens. Rode off then. . . ."

Ragan's eyes were still on the hills. At the fading of Pogue's voice, he came around. Buckman's eyes were closed and he was breathing hard and near exhaustion, but he was a stubborn man and not yet ready to die.

"Korello . . . he been with Chandler long?"

"Not long. Couple of months, a bit more."

"Sounds like this Chandler maybe brought him in for something special."

Ann was looking closely at Ragan's set features. "This Korello, he mean something to you?"

"We've met," Dan replied with a shrug. "Plenty fast with a gun."

"Wouldn't make no difference whether he was or wasn't," Pogue muttered. "Ain't no way I can buck him, laying here, flat on my back. . . ."

Ragan's shoulder again stirred. "No use you even trying. Thing to do is get help, get that lawman over here. You've got some proof now. That bullet you took, shape the place is in. Be glad to stop in Mason City, tell him all about it, and get him started. . . ."

The sudden, sharp *crackle* of gunfire, the dull *thud* of bullets driving into the walls of the house, broke into Dan Ragan's words. Abruptly his jaw set and a bleakness came over his features. Drawing his pistol, he wheeled to the doorway.

"Reckon they changed their minds," he said, and turned into the hallway.

VI

Ragan pointed for the back entrance to the house, altered his thinking, and, crossing the kitchen, entered the room adjoining it on the east. It was Earl's quarters, apparently, judging from the clothing and other articles that could only belong to the boy. Moving to the solitary window, he drew up close, peered out.

He located Dave Yates at once—off his horse and crouching behind a good-size cottonwood beyond the edge of the yard. While he watched, Yates glanced to his left. Twisting about, Dan saw that Yates was watching Steve Denver working himself around, under cover of the weeds, to where he could cover the side of the house not visible to him.

Suddenly the cowpuncher's voice rode across the hot silence. "You Buckmans . . . there in the house!"

Dan doubled back to the kitchen door, anger and frustration tearing at him as he realized that he had been sucked into a situation he had sought desperately to avoid. Reaching the opening, he looked toward the cottonwood.

"What do you want?"

"Just aiming to let you know we're back," Yates answered. "Me 'n' the boys."

"Am I supposed to write that down or something?"

"Just keep remembering it in case you all decide to pull out. Too late now for that. Sent a couple of the boys you potted for the boss. Figured we'd better hang around, be sure you'd wait."

Ragan, hunched in the doorway, leveled his pistol at the base of the thick tree behind which Yates was hiding, and pressed off a shot. The rider jumped back, yelled in surprise. Dan laughed.

"Just want you to know you'll be waiting right where you are now for a spell, too. Try moving out from behind that cottonwood and you're a dead man."

Yates had no reply, but the toes of his boots, visible earlier, were now well withdrawn. Rising, Dan turned, saw Earl standing in the center of the kitchen. The boy had witnessed the entire incident and his eyes were bright with fresh hope.

"What you said, that mean you're staying?"

Ragan gave him a half smile, not sure in his own mind yet. If there were only Yates and Denver watching the house, he could probably slip by them, be on his way long before Chandler and the rest of his bully boys could make it back. Still. . . .

"There a room at the other end of the house?"

Earl bobbed his head quickly. "My sister's," he said, and led the way down the narrow corridor, past Pogue's quarters, to a door at the extreme end.

Opening it, Dan entered, crossed to the curtained window in the far wall. Drawing it aside carefully, he probed the yard with his eyes. It took a minute or two of painstaking search but he finally located Denver. The rider had stationed himself in a shallow arroyo that curved across the upper end of Buckman's yard.

Dan gave that thought. The place was completely under the eyes of the two men. Yates could see the back door, the north and east walls of the house, as well as most of the yard that lay on the west. Hiding in the wash, Steve Denver had a good view of the structure's south side along with a fair command of the yard, also.

Muttering a soft curse, Ragan slid the window open, prepared to throw a bullet at Denver just to let the rider know he had been spotted, and then lowered his weapon. Let Denver believe he had not been located; it could prove to be an advantage later.

Turning, Dan moved back to the bedroom where Pogue Buckman lay. Ann was sitting on the edge of the bed, his limp hand in hers. The wounded man appeared much weaker now, and Dan guessed all the talking he had done had taken a heavy toll of his strength.

The rancher looked up as Ragan entered, a wan smile on his lips. Sweat had gathered on his brow and he made a gesture at brushing it off.

"Got us boxed in, eh?" he said in a low voice. "Well, I ain't through yet. Give me my rifle . . . prop me up so's I can see . . . and I'll. . . ."

"Not that easy," Ragan snapped. "Couple other people here that'll get killed if you try making a fight of it."

Pogue made a slight motion with his hand. "Of course. Wasn't thinking straight. Only about my land."

"If you're thinking of Earl and me," Ann said in a hurried voice, "don't worry. We'll manage, somehow."

"That's fool talk!" Ragan shot back. "There'll be a dozen men out there . . . maybe more. And they'll all be shooting. In an hour's time you'll all be dead and this place will be ashes."

The girl's mouth opened and a shudder passed through her. Pogue Buckman frowned, mustered up a look of anger. "No need for that kind of. . . ."

"There's plenty need for it!" Dan snarled. "It's about time somebody better be making sense here. You people don't seem to realize what you're up against! Facts are facts, and there's no way of getting around them."

Ann turned to Ragan. "If you mean, about Pogue, I know. I may be strange to this country, this life, but I'm no child."

Earl moved quickly to the side of the bed, his young face strained. "You mean that it's worse than you let on . . . that maybe you're going to . . . to . . . ?"

"Die," Pogue Buckman finished for him. "Good chance of it, boy. Only don't give up yet. I'm not. Think I'm even surprising our friend Ragan."

Dan nodded. "Got to admit you're fooling me and holding out better than I figured. Could be your insides aren't as torn up as we thought."

"Then there is a chance?" Ann asked eagerly.

"Maybe, if we had a doctor, or could get him to one. That means Mason City . . . same as for the sheriff."

Dan glanced toward the window. The late morning heat was beginning to make itself felt inside the house. He sleeved the sweat from his face, shook his head.

"Best thing we could all do is get out of here."

"We?" Ann echoed the word.

"Hell, I'm trapped in here same as you. I try making a run for it, I could stop a few bullets."

For a long minute he stood there, anger bright in his brooding eyes, and then he shrugged, almost as if embarrassed. "Sorry for how I'm talking. No fault of yours I'm here. I didn't have to horn in, but I did, so all I can do is make the best of it." He glanced down at Pogue. "You fixed pretty good on ammunition for that rifle I saw in the kitchen?"

"You aim to fight?"

"Don't see as we've got a choice."

"Reckon not. Forty, maybe fifty rounds for the rifle. No more'n that. There's a shotgun in the closet. Couple a dozen shells for it. Best I can do."

He had his own six-gun and the loops on his belt were almost all filled. There were spare cartridges in his saddlebags—if he could get to the bay. In all he guessed he had about fifty rounds. Not too bad a shape for bullets.

"How long you think we can hold out?" Pogue wondered, bolstering his strength with another drink of rye.

"Not long. Be a matter of keeping Chandler and his outfit at their distance until dark. Then they'll likely pull back until daylight. Help could be here by then."

"Help? Who?" Ann said hurriedly.

"The sheriff and maybe a couple or three deputies." Dan

swung to Earl. "You ride a horse?"

"Sure. Done plenty of riding."

"Know the way to Mason City?"

"Gone there two, three times with Pogue. Can do it easy."

Ann was shaking her head. "No. I won't let him go. Those men out there, they'll not let him get out of the yard."

"I'll take care of them," Dan said. He turned to the boy again. "Means a hard ride . . . hard and fast all the way. You get there, tell the sheriff what's happening, tell him to get some men and come fast. Then look up the doctor. We want him here, too."

Ann's eyes were bright with fear and worry. Pogue reached out, took her hand in his. "Our only chance," he murmured. "And the boy can do it."

She brushed nervously at her lips. "I . . . I don't know. I'm afraid of those men out there, waiting with guns. . . ."

"Ragan'll see to them."

Dan moved toward the door. "Going to leave this up to you. If you figure it's too big a risk for the boy to take, be all right with me. We'll just fight it out and hope things'll work our way."

"I can do it . . . easy," Earl insisted. "And it won't take me long. I can use the sorrel."

"If you decide to go, you'll use my horse," Ragan said. "He's fast and plenty strong. Besides, he's handy. Be no trouble getting to him. While you're thinking it over, I'll have a look outside."

He walked from the room, made his way to Earl's quarters off the kitchen. Moving to the window, he turned his attention to the cottonwood tree. The tip of Dave Yates's shoulder was visible. The man had not changed positions, evidently electing to believe the warning Dan had served. Drawing back, he returned to the kitchen, halted in its center as Earl came suddenly from Pogue's bedroom into the hall.

Seeing Ragan, the boy slowed briefly, dug at his eyes with a knuckle, and then drew himself up to full height. "Reckon I'm ready to go," he said.

VII

Dan's gaze shifted beyond the boy to Ann Buckman, standing now in the doorway of Pogue's room. Her face was taut, worried, but she nodded slightly, signifying consent of her brother and herself.

Ragan took the boy by the arm, guided him to the window of the adjoining room. Pointing to the cottonwood, he said: "Yates is behind that tree. He's the one we've got to fool."

Earl was pale but his lips were firm. "Expect I could crawl along the house till I got to them tall weeds. Then I. . . ."

"Won't be able to do that. You'll be leading my horse."

"Then how'll I get by him?"

"I'll draw his attention, keep him busy. You wait here in the doorway. Keep down low, out of sight. When I give you the signal, move fast. Grab the reins of my horse, lead him across the yard to the barn. Once you're there, mount up and head out. Don't run him. Hold him to a walk for the first quarter mile so's Yates or Denver won't hear you leaving, then make him give you all he's got. Understand?"

Earl swallowed hard, said: "Yes, sir."

"You remember what to tell the sheriff?"

"To get here quick with some men. Then I'm to find the doctor, tell him to come, too."

"Fine. Guess you're all set then."

"Yes, sir, I'm ready."

Dan squeezed the boy's arm, grinned, and stepped up to the doorway. Hunched low, he moved out onto the porch, halted. Yates had seen him, had pulled himself in tighter behind the tree. Likely he was leveling his pistol at that very moment, expecting Ragan to enter the yard.

Dan glanced over his shoulder at Earl as he drew his own weapon. "When I jump off this porch and start shooting, make your move. Good luck."

He waited for no reply from the boy, simply thumbed back the hammer of his .45, pointed it at the cottonwood, and lunged into the yard. He saw Yates make a move to fire an answering shot, sent another bullet at the man, drove him again behind the tree's trunk as he legged it for the woodpile.

Reaching the shelter of the logs and dry branches, he ducked in low and fired a third bullet at Yates, keeping him pinned down as he swung his attention to the barn. Earl was already swinging up onto the bay. He'd made it with no trouble. Now, if he remembered to ride out slowly and quietly. . . .

Bullets *thudded* into the woodpile. Ragan came up with a jerk, threw himself back farther into the mound of firewood. Low to the ground he looked through a small opening at the cottonwood. Yates had not moved, he noted as he punched out the empties in the pistol's cylinder and reloaded. Denver had changed, however; he had abandoned his position in the arroyo, was now hunkered behind a mound of rock and dirt only a few strides from his partner.

The plan to get Earl out of the yard and on his way to Mason City had worked fine; the problem he faced now was how to make it back to the house with a whole skin. Both Denver and Yates were in position to cut down on him the instant he stepped into the open.

Twisting about, he gave his surroundings swift appraisal. Immediately behind him stood the remains of an old corral, apparently unused for some time. The cross logs were old, sagged heavily, and were probably destined to become firewood in the near future. There was some degree of protection there—but not much.

A short way below it he could see the wagon shed, a fairly

large structure open on three sides. A dusty, two-seated surrey was the only occupant. Dan considered the area thoughtfully; if he could make it to the old corral without catching a bullet, he could then drop back behind the wagon shed and find refuge.

From that point, assuming he could keep the two men pinned down in their present locations, he could cut across behind the feed shed, reach the barn and its nearby corrals, and quickly move on to the main house.

There were a lot of ifs involved, he thought, swiveling his attention back to Yates and Steve Denver, but it was a risk he'd have to take as it was imperative he get back inside the house. If Chandler and his bunch trapped him in the yard, not only would he be unable to help the Buckmans, but his own life wouldn't be worth a plugged copper.

That thought brought the reminder of a different sort of threat to mind—Jody Strickland. Glancing up the slope to the trail he had been following when the gunshots halted him, he studied the dull gray and sage green of the growth covering the small plateau. There was no sign of life, of movement. *Give him time,* Ragan told himself silently. *He'll come. He'll never quit.*

Brushing at the sweat on his face, Dan turned to the moment. Yates was saying something to Denver, calling his words across the narrow distance that separated them in a voice purposely lowered to keep others from hearing. Checking his pistol to assure himself that it was fully loaded, Ragan backed slowly to the extreme end of the woodpile, paused. He looked again toward the cottonwood and the mound of earth where the two men waited. They had not moved, and no longer were talking. This would be the hardest point, the most dangerous, those moments during which he crossed to the crumbling old corral and thence to the wagon shed. He'd have little protection—and two guns, not one, would be reaching for his life.

Taking a deep breath, he crouched low, and then, snapping a

quick shot at Steve Denver, the greatest threat at that particular point, he lunged for the scanty protection of the sagging logs.

Instantly Yates opened up. Lead *thudded* into the rotting wood, *spanged* off the edges with a high, whining sound. Dan threw himself forward, went full-length to the ground. Now Denver's gun had begun to crackle but his shots were coming too late. The few moments of time during which he'd been driven to cover had made the difference.

Ragan lay quietly, breathing deeply, slowly gathering his wind. The shooting ceased, and, rolling to his side, he looked through the cross work of logs toward the cottonwood. Yates and Denver had stayed put—neither man wanting to risk themselves now since they were unsure of his exact position.

Dan sighed softly. He hadn't expected his luck to run that well. Rolling onto his belly, he pivoted about to where he faced the wagon shed. It was a long fifty feet away, and he couldn't hope to keep his movements hidden as he crossed the open ground.

Slowly he drew himself to his knees and hands, finally to where he was on his feet, bent forward, poised like a runner about to begin a race. Abruptly he leaped forward and, hunched low, broke into an erratic, zigzagging run for the shelter of the wagon shed.

Immediately both Yates and Denver began to shoot. Bullets whipped past Ragan, dug sand about his pounding feet, ricocheted off nearby rocks to sign shrilly into space. He felt something pluck at his sleeve, tug at the brim of his hat. Suddenly pain in his leg brought an oath to his lips, caused him to break stride. He'd been hit. For an instant he thought he was going down, but he fought the weakness savagely, caught himself, and plunged on.

He was behind the thick plank wall of the shed, sucking hard for breath, swearing steadily at the misfortune of having gotten himself shot—of allowing himself to get drawn into something that was none of his business in the first place. But it was no time for hashing things over; he was in it, and Dave Yates and Steve Denver could decide to press their advantage if they were aware that he'd been winged.

Still low, ignoring the pain in his leg, he crossed behind the wagon shed. A wedge-shaped patch of shoulder-high rabbit brush grew off the end of the building, and, moving as hurriedly as possible, he made his way through the tough growth to where he was behind the corral on the south side of the yard, and at its upper end.

From the cottonwood came the muffled voice of Steve Denver as he placed a question to his partner.

"Can't tell," Yates's answer was plain. "Last I seen, he was ducking in behind the wagon shed. Ain't so sure he was hit. You figure he was?"

Denver made his reply to that, and then once more Yates's words carried to Dan. "Circle around, what we'd best do. You take that side, I'll go this'n. Maybe we can corner him back there. Now, keep your eyes peeled."

Dan Ragan frowned, again swiped at the sweat clothing his face. He was on a direct line with the back door of the Buckman house, only a few yards distant. Both men could see him when he emerged from the weeds, if they happened to be looking in that direction. But if he remained there, one or both, doubling back along the edge of the yard, were sure to spot him. Once more it was a matter of no choice.

Holstering his pistol, and clapping a hand to the steadily bleeding wound in his thigh, he went to his boot toes and darted across the narrow strip of open ground to the porch running the width of the structure. Stepping up onto it, he leaned against the door frame while he recovered his breath. Dave Yates's voice came to him.

"All right, you ready?"

Denver's reply was audible from that nearer position. "Reckon so. But I ain't so sure it's smart. That bird's a real heller with that iron he packs."

Ragan grinned in relief. They hadn't seen him cross over.

VIII

Ann Buckman, standing just inside the door, stepped back quickly as he entered the kitchen, her eyes on the bloody wound in his leg. She opened her mouth to speak but he shook off her concern, continued on to the window in Earl's room. There was a good possibility he might be afforded a clear shot at Yates or Denver from that point, since they would be moving across the yard; if he could lower the odds a bit more, all the better.

He could not see either man. Apparently they were being cautious, taking no chances, which would further indicate that they were still unsure of his whereabouts. They'd be somewhere beyond the edge of the yard, he guessed—one on either side and keeping below the weedy berm and behind the thick brush. The kitchen just might offer a better view.

Pulling back from the window, he wheeled, forgetful of his wound, and went to one knee as a stab of pain cut the leg out from under him. Muttering under his breath, he pulled himself upright, returned to the kitchen. Ann, watching it all from a corner of the room, met him with an angry frown.

"I want you to sit down, let me do something for that leg. Maybe I don't know exactly what, but you can tell me."

"Not much more'n a scratch," he said, halting in the doorway. "Best I keep a sharp eye on the outside."

There still was no sign of the two men. Ragan rubbed at his chin, considering that. If they figured him to be somewhere around the wagon shed, at least one of them would be visible as he worked his way in from the side, assuming the other halted at a vantage point to wait with a drawn pistol. Unless. . . .

Pivoting, this time with more care, he walked the length of the hallway, entered Ann's room, and stepped up to the window. He glanced out, saw that he had guessed correctly. Steve Denver was back in the arroyo. He had decided against having his look at the back side of the wagon shed. That could mean Dave Yates was on his own.

At once Ragan retraced his steps to the room that adjoined the kitchen and, ignoring Ann's stern frown, crowded up close to the window, placed his eyes on the big cottonwood. Yates was not there. Then his glance picked up motion a bit farther to the left where a distinct hump in the land created a sort of sink behind it. It was Yates. He had forsaken the cottonwood for a more comfortable, as well as safer, location.

Dan gave it all deep thought. Since both men had chosen not to press the hunt, it could only mean that they expected Ross Chandler and the rest of his crew to put in an appearance shortly. They saw no reason to expose themselves when help, in force, was imminent.

Some of the hard tension slipped from Dan Ragan's shoulders at that realization. He could forget them for the time being, start making whatever preparations he could against the time when Chandler's outfit struck. The important thing was that Earl had slipped out of the yard unnoticed, and was now well on his way to Mason City. It was just a matter of holding out until the law could arrive.

That could take some doing. It would be he—he alone against Chandler and however many riders he brought with him. Pogue Buckman was in no condition to help, nor was Ann, who probably had never fired a gun in her life. He shifted wearily, winced as his bad leg took his weight briefly, and returned to the kitchen. Grasping the top rung of a ladder-back chair, he dragged it up to where he could look through the doorway and have a full view of the yard, and then settled down. Getting things ready for the siege would have to wait a few minutes. He had to have a few minutes' rest.

"Now can I do something about your leg?"

He had all but forgotten Ann. She was still in the corner, waiting patiently. He nodded slightly, said: "How's your brother?"

"Sleeping now," she answered as she crossed to the stove where a pan of water was simmering. Taking it up, she placed it on the floor beside his chair, and faced him. "He's much weaker, I think, in spite of the whiskey. There's no chance for him, is there . . . ?"

She didn't put it in the form of a question but as a statement of fact. Dan shrugged. "He's strong . . . stronger than I figured."

"But that's not enough. He can't hold out until the doctor gets here . . . not until tomorrow."

Ragan made no comment, allowing her to shape her own confirming conclusions. He had obtained his knife from a side pocket, had opened the blade, and was slitting the cloth of his breeches so as to expose the wound. It was not serious, as he had guessed; the bullet had slashed across the outer surface of the leg, laying open a shallow gash that bled copiously. It would be sore as hell for a few days and likely would cause some stiffness, but properly dressed it would be nothing to worry about.

"Any of that whiskey left?" he asked.

Ann rose immediately, went to Pogue's bedroom, and returned at once with the bottle. It was still a third full. He took it from her, making his thanks, and said: "Could use some of those clean rags."

She stepped to a cabinet in the adjoining room, procured a white square of cotton, and, without saying anything to him, tore it into strips. Taking one, she soaked it in the hot water, knelt beside him, and cleaned away the dried blood surrounding the wound. That completed, she drew back, glanced at the bottle in his hand.

Ragan tipped it first to his lips, took a healthy swallow, and then, bracing himself, poured a quantity into the raw opening carved by the bullet. A mumbled oath escaped his lips and the corners of his jaws showed white for an instant, and then he eased back, setting the bottle aside.

"Could use a bit of salve," he murmured, brushing at the sweat on his forehead. "Keeps the bandage from sticking."

She brought him a jar of some home-concocted remedy, a thick, gray-looking ointment that smelled strongly of sassafras. He smeared a coating over the wound, wrapped a strip of bandage about the leg, and carefully secured the loose end, making certain it would not come loose at some inopportune moment and create a problem.

"Expect that does the job," he said, rising and testing the leg. There was a slight stab of pain and stiffness was already setting in, but it would be no great hindrance. "Obliged to you."

Ann was gathering up the left-over bandages, the pan of water, and jar of ointment. She smiled, and he turned away, moved quietly down the hall. Reaching Buckman's door, he glanced in. The wounded man was still sleeping, but it was not a good sleep, was instead that of the dying. In no more than an hour's time there had been a vast change in the man—one for the worse.

Continuing on into Ann's room, he crossed to the window. Steve Denver was still in the dry wash. Doubling back over his tracks to the room adjoining the kitchen, he made his check of Yates. Dave had not moved, either, was laying in the shallow bowl behind the pile of earth and rock. When was Ross Chandler coming?

It was noon, possibly a little later. He doubted Chandler's ranch was more than a two- or three-hour ride. What was holding him back? The only answer Dan could come up with was that the rancher had not been on hand when his men rode in. If they were forced to wait. . . .

"Are you hungry?"

Ann's voice brought him from his thoughts. "Not 'specially."

"There's plenty of that broth. And the coffee's ready. I could fry you a steak."

"Broth and coffee'll do fine."

She turned to the stove, which was making of the room a heated, airless oven, and began to fill a bowl with the thick soup. He settled down at the table, shifting it about slightly so that he could watch the yard.

He should be getting the weapons and ammunition Pogue Buckman owned together where all would be handy, he thought, again aware of an earlier warning that he should be making preparations. He would, just as soon as he had some of the broth and coffee. One thing, he'd forgotten to get the extra cartridges for his six-gun from his saddlebags before Earl had left. He guessed maybe it didn't matter too much. Holding back Chandler was going to involve more bluffing than shooting, anyway.

He leaned back as Ann came up, placed the bowl of steaming, yellow soup before him, along with a plate of fresh bread. He began to eat, more from necessity than from any actual desire. He finished off the soup under the serious, watchful eyes of Ann, turned then to the coffee she had provided.

It was black, strong, and to his liking. He grinned his appreciation to her, said: "Not many can make coffee this good. Same goes for the soup. Obliged to you."

"It's you that is to be thanked. If you hadn't come by when you did, stopped to help. . . ."

Ragan's eyes were on the yard, his thoughts on Jody Strickland. During the heat of the last hour or so of action, that problem had slipped from his mind. Now he was remembering, realizing the boy was drawing nearer with each passing moment. It was entirely possible he was somewhere in the Lagrima Valley at that very instant of thought.

"You're wondering about that man, the one who wants to kill you."

Dan stirred, shifted his gaze to his empty cup. Ann reached for the pot, refilled the container.

"Isn't there some way you can talk to him, make him understand?" she asked.

"Tried that. Wasn't interested in listening."

She shook her head. "What is it that is making him that way? Why is he so determined to shoot you?"

Ragan's moody eyes were again reaching through the doorway to the yard, to the buildings there, to the land beyond.

"Was it over a woman?"

He nodded slowly. "A woman . . . yes, but one he hardly knew. Was his stepmother. He was 'most grown when his pa married her."

Ann studied him with quiet intent. Small patches of sweat glistened on her cheeks and her eyes seemed a deeper blue in the confines of the heat-laden room.

"And you loved her, but she married him . . . ?"

Once more he moved restlessly on his chair. "Guess you could say that, only. . . ."

The hard, fast drum of hoofs in the yard brought him up short. Almost lazily he got to his feet.

"Company we've been expecting's here," he said in a level, unhurried voice. "Want you to bring me the guns and ammunition Pogue was talking about, put it all here on the table. Then find yourself a corner and sit down. You're to keep low . . . don't want a stray bullet hitting you."

IX

The *thudding* sound of the oncoming horses, the shouts of Chandler's men filled the room. For a long, breathless moment Ann Buckman stood rigid, paralyzed by fear. And then, reassured by Ragan's calm, almost indifferent manner, she spun, raced off down the hall.

Dan, hunched low, moved to the doorway, threw his glance to the low spot where Dave Yates was hiding. Six riders were in plain view, making no effort to conceal their presence. This would be Ross Chandler's method of showing his disdain for the Buckmans.

Ragan studied the men. Chandler would be the one in the center—the one doing all the talking to Yates, still not visible. The rancher appeared to be squat, with a ruddy face and an angry way of chewing on the cigar clenched between his teeth. He wore ordinary range clothing: corded pants, dark, coarse woven shirt, wide-brimmed hat, and scarred boots. A pair of leather chaps were draped across the saddle of the tall sorrel he rode. A working rancher, Dan thought, and not one of those who sit it out in a rocking chair raising cattle from the comfort of their front porch.

He heard a noise behind him, looked back, saw Ann had gathered together the rifle and shotgun and all the ammunition Pogue Buckman had mentioned. As she set the last of it on the table, he nodded.

"Best you stay down now, like I said . . . in case shooting starts."

"I'll be with my brother," she replied, her lips tight, and turned away.

Buckman's room wouldn't be the safest place in the house since it fronted on the yard, and Ragan doubted the plank walls would stop bullets at close range. But the girl seemed to have her mind set on it.

"Can think of better places," he said, "but have it your own way. Get down flat on the floor if they open up."

She gave no indication that she heard, continued on. Ragan brought his attention back to Chandler and the others, still in conversation. Dave Yates, looking somewhat downcast, had come from his hiding place and was mounting his horse. Steve Denver rode into the party, halted. It would seem that both had come in for a chiding from the rancher, probably for taking such pains to avoid what he considered persons of no consequence.

Abruptly the riders moved away from the sink beyond the mound, and abreast, walking their horses, entered Buckman's yard. In a spaced, half circle line, they drew up, facing the back door of the house.

"Buckman!"

Chandler's tone was arrogant, impatient, depicting a man accustomed to having his way and getting things on his own terms. There were a lot of Ross Chandlers in the West, Dan realized. Pirates, plunderers—out to make kings of themselves.

"Buckman, if you ain't dead, show yourself!"

Evidently the rancher had been told by Yates and the others that Pogue had been shot down, likely had been killed. Chandler was feeling his way, testing his ground before making any drastic moves that might prove unnecessary. If Pogue Buckman were dead, matters would be simple for him; he'd just close in, take over from Ann Buckman and her young brother on any terms he saw fit.

"Buckman! You coming out . . . or am I coming in?"

Dan Ragan, arms folded across his chest, stepped out onto the porch, doing it slowly and with deliberate unconcern. Yates stiffened, said something under his breath to the rancher.

Ross Chandler leaned forward, forearms resting on the horn of his saddle. He fixed his small, hard eyes on Ragan. "So you're the handy-andy that's shooting up my boys. . . ."

Dan swept the line of men with his glance, nodded coolly. "Be a couple more carrying lead if they don't get their minds changed quick."

The two cowpunchers at the ends of the row abruptly ceased their stealthy shifting about. Chandler chomped his cigar angrily.

"Just who the hell are you? Some kin of these jacklegs? Brother, maybe?"

"Been asked that before. Still don't see that it cuts any ice."

"Then what right've you got horning in . . . ?"

"Same right that says you can hooraw these folks around, kill off their stock, drive them off their land."

"Offered to buy!"

"And I reckon all the things your bunch've been doing was just to help them make up their minds."

Chandler swore hotly, spat. "This ain't none of your say-so anyway. I'm dealing with Pogue Buckman . . . nobody else. Trot him out here where we can do some talking or I'll figure he ain't around no more to deal. . . ."

"You're still wasting your breath, Ross," Buckman said from the doorway.

Masking his surprise, Dan wheeled slowly. Pogue was leaning against the door frame. Directly behind him, unseen from the yard, was Ann supporting him as best she could with her hands braced under his armpits.

Chandler swore again, swung impatiently to Yates. "I thought you told me . . . ," he snarled, and then stopped. For a long minute he sat quietly on the big sorrel, eyes locked on the horn of the fancy, double-rigged saddle he was forking. Finally he brushed at the sweat on his face and looked up.

"Tried doing this the easy way, Buckman. Made you a fair offer for your place but you're too jugheaded to listen."

"Not that. Just don't want to sell. Built this place up and I aim to hang onto it . . . keep it going. Got good reason . . . now. Ross, don't you be forgetting . . . what the sheriff told you last time. . . ."

Chandler made an impatient gesture with his hand. "Was a long time ago. I can deal with McGaffey."

Dan looked closely at Buckman. The man was on his feet by the grace of sheer nerve and raw whiskey. But he wouldn't be able to put up his bold front much longer.

"Law's the same," he said, taking up the conversation in hopes of sparing Buckman as much strain as possible. "Nothing's changed. Man says his place is not for sale, and means it. Law tells him he can say no to anybody he wants."

"Only thing," Chandler said, cocking his head to one side, "I ain't much of a hand for taking no for an answer."

"Reckon you'd better get used to it, because that's the way it is here. What's got you so set for this place anyway? You've got plenty of room across the front to make your drives, and nobody's ever going to stop you."

"Ain't a case of needing it. Just that it sets right in the middle of my property, cuts it in two. Don't favor that kind of a set-up."

"You talk to Buckman about selling out before you bought the place below him?"

Chandler looked mildly surprised as if wondering how Ragan would be in possession of that bit of information. But he passed it off, shrugged.

"Ain't never been in the habit of talking over my business with the neighbors."

"Reckon you should've this time. Might've saved yourself and other folks a heap of trouble, because he could have told you then he wouldn't sell. But I expect it wouldn't've made no difference . . . never does to jaspers like you."

"You're dead right," Chandler said, "it sure wouldn't. But I ain't here to jaw with some saddle bum. Buckman, I'm giving you your last chance. You willing to show sense, come to terms?"

Pogue's face was slack and his skin was the color of a campfire's cold ashes. His eyes seemed to have receded deeply into his skull.

"Not . . . selling."

Ross Chandler spurred forward, anger ripping at his ruddy features. "God dammit, Buckman, if you think I'm letting you. . . ."

Dan Ragan took a long, sliding step forward. His arm barely moved but suddenly his gun was in his hand. The weapon slapped hard into the heated silence and a spurt of dust showered the front hoofs of Chandler's sorrel. The big horse shied off, reared.

Chandler shouted an oath. The rider to his left surged forward, hand dragging at the weapon on his hip. Ragan's pistol *cracked* again. The cowpuncher buckled forward, a puzzled frown on his leathery face as he tumbled from the saddle.

Ragan, his eyes small, sharp points of granite flicking back and forth over the remaining men, challenging, daring, settled his gaze finally upon Chandler.

"What's it going to take to convince you, mister?"

The cigar was gone from the rancher's teeth. There was a stillness upon his features, almost an expression of shock. But when he spoke, directing his words to Pogue Buckman, his voice was level.

"All right, this is what you want. You remember, howsomever, I can bring in gun slicks, too."

"You . . . always had them," Buckman said slowly. "No surprise."

"Tried to be reasonable. Now you're forcing my hand, making me do something I don't want. . . ."

"Buckman's through talking," Ragan cut in, moving to the

edge of the porch. "He's given you his answer, so load up your boys and get out."

Chandler flushed as his mouth tightened. "You giving me orders. . . ."

"I am. Get off Buckman range and stay off. Goes for you and every man working for you. If this place ever goes up for sale, you'll get first crack. Until then, you'll find it healthy to forget about buying . . . or stealing . . . it. That clear?"

Chandler glared at Ragan for several hushed moments, and then abruptly jerked the sorrel about. He made a motion at two of his men. Both rode forward, dismounted, and draped the dead cowpuncher crosswise upon his saddle. Silently they went back onto their mounts, resumed their positions in the half circle.

Once more the rancher faced Dan Ragan. "You're figuring you've got the whip handle now. Maybe . . . but don't do no crowing. I'll be back."

"Sort of guessed you would. Your kind never learns."

"Your kind don't, either! If you're smart, you'll hightail it out of here before I come back . . . sundown."

"Why wait?" Ragan said mildly. "You know Buckman's answer . . . and where you stand."

"Giving him a chance to get some sense, change his mind."

Ragan laughed. "What you're meaning to say is you'll feel safer with a fast gun like Jim Korello siding you and helping you ramrod this deal along."

Chandler's face darkened. His eyes sparked, and, swinging the sorrel around sharply, he said—"You got till sundown."—and led his men out of the yard.

X

A gasp from Ann brought Ragan around swiftly. He crossed the porch in a single stride, reached out, caught Pogue Buckman just as the man began to fall. Taking him in his arms, Dan carried him to his quarters, laid him on the bed.

Reaching for the bottle of rye, he pressed the opening between Pogue's lips, forced him to drink. "Took one hell of a man to do what he did," he murmured, glancing at Ann.

"You think he fooled Chandler?"

"Sure of it. And he bought us some time."

Buckman stirred, choking a little on the liquor, opened his eyes.

Dan set the bottle back on the table, grinned down at him. "Next time you decide to take a walk, let me know. I'll go along."

Buckman moved his head slightly. "Had to do something. Not right . . . you out there carrying my load."

"I tried to keep him from it," Ann murmured. "Only he wouldn't listen. Said he had to do it."

Dan reached for her hand and, unseen by Pogue, squeezed it gently, assuring her that it didn't matter, that to permit the man to have his way was the best favor they could bestow. He had felt a need to defy Ross Chandler for one final time and in so doing had satisfied some pressing, inner demand.

Ann leaned over the bed, fussed briefly with the clean shirt she had provided for him, and the bandage underneath it. He had buttoned it collar high to conceal any evidence of his wound.

"Is there anything I can get you, Pogue?" she asked as she finished.

"Nothing. Seem sort of sleepy. Expect I'm needing . . . rest." His wavering eves settled on Dan. "Any word from the sheriff . . . or Earl?"

"Not yet. Too early. Take yourself a nap. Time you wake up they may be here."

Pogue sighed contentedly, closed his lids. Dan backed quietly for the door, made his way to the kitchen, leaving Ann with her brother. Presently she joined him.

"He went straight to sleep," she said, dropping into one of the chairs. "Tired from what he did, I suppose."

"Something he figured he had to do. Happens to a man now and then. Price doesn't matter."

"I know it hurt him terribly. I'm afraid now that it will. . . ." Her voice broke off.

Ragan stepped up close, put his hands upon her shoulders, and pressed her head against his body.

"Don't begrudge him those few minutes. Was proving something to himself, I expect. Maybe that he was as much a man as the next one. No difference in the end, anyway. What's another hour if he got peace of mind out of it?"

"But it solved nothing, not the slightest thing!" Ann said, pulling back. "We've still got to face that . . . that terrible man, Chandler, and his outlaws! He'll return, just like he said he would . . . and this time he won't just talk. He'll have more men with him and they'll. . . ."

"We know that. Pogue doesn't," Ragan broke in firmly. "Let's keep it that way."

"He was standing there, heard. . . ."

"Don't think he understood anything that was said there at the last. All that stuck in his mind is that he told Ross Chandler off, turned him away."

"But what can we do when Chandler comes at sundown?"

He rubbed at the corners of his chin. "Something we'd best get figured out."

Ann rose, walked to the door, stared out across the yard. Beyond the hard pack the green of the trees and lesser growth appeared gray in the afternoon's heat haze.

"What you said about Earl and the sheriff, that wasn't true, was it? They couldn't return that soon."

"Tomorrow morning, I'd guess. If it makes Pogue feel better, thinking they're not far off, let him." Dan paused, studied the soft contours of the girl's face turned partly from him. "You know he'll not see the sun set, don't you?"

She whirled to him, eyes filled with grief, a sob tearing from her throat. "I . . . I guess I do, only I can't seem to admit it to myself!" she cried, and in a sudden burst of emotion ran to him.

He took her awkwardly in his arms, a man always ill at ease in such moments, and with one hand stroked her hair gently. He was at a loss for words and so they stood in silence, the sweltering stillness in the room broken only by her weeping.

Eventually it was past and she drew back, wiping at her eyes with a small square of handkerchief taken from the pocket of her dress.

"I'm sorry," she murmured. "I shouldn't let myself go like that, acting as if I were a child."

"Best thing you could do . . . get it out," Ragan said, moving to the doorway where it was cooler. "Makes it easier to think straight. Something you've got to do."

She looked up at him, puzzled. "I'm not sure I know what you mean."

"Just this. Place will be yours. Probably by the time Chandler comes back. Up to you now to decide what you want to do."

Ann's lips parted and shock filled her eyes at his blunt words—and at the realization that he was speaking the truth.

"I guess I never gave that any thought."

"Understand that easy enough. But it's a fact. Be up to you whether you sell out to Chandler or stay on and fight."

"Half will be Earl's. He ought to have some say in it."

"Tomorrow'll be too late for Chandler. He's coming today . . . late . . . and he means to settle things one way or another."

Ann stared at the floor, mind wrestling with the problem. She looked up suddenly, faced him. "What do you think I ought to do?"

He shifted on his feet, placed his shoulders to the door frame. "Hard thing for me to answer. Never was much on letting anybody run over me. Be different where you're concerned. Hard for a woman and a boy to fight an outfit like Chandler's. You'd need help, good help, and plenty of it."

"But the law. . . ."

"Sure, but you can see how that is. It'll protect you if it's around . . . only it's not. Long day's ride from here, and that sort of drops things right into the hands of men like Chandler, fixes it so's they can do just about what pleases them . . . and to hell with everybody else."

"If I went to the law, made some charges against him, they'd have to do something."

"You've got to have proof against the Chandlers, and they're good at seeing you never find any. Nobody around here would have the guts to come out against him, stand by you."

"Not even you, Dan?"

He gave her an odd smile. "Doubt if what I'd say would be worth much far as the law goes. Not much but a drifter, passing through . . . that's what they'd say. And there's other reasons."

"That man chasing you, wanting to kill you for what you did to his father, that what you mean?"

"Part of it."

She moved into the doorway, features thoughtful as she gazed into the yard. "Pogue's worked so hard to make a home for us . . . for all of us. Wanted us to have a good place to live, a real home. That's something we missed. Our folks died when Earl was just a baby. We've had a sort of pillar to post existence ever since. But we managed to stay together and keep things going. I became a schoolteacher, and Pogue came out here when he was offered a good job on a ranch. It turned out better than he'd hoped. The man he worked for tired of ranching and sold the place . . . this place . . . to him for almost nothing. I continued to teach while Earl did odd jobs in the town where we lived, waiting for Pogue to get things all set for us. When he finally was ready, he sent word to us and we took the money we'd managed to save and moved here. To what we thought would be a wonderful home . . . a new life. Now"—Ann paused, shrugged disconsolately—"it's ending like this. All for nothing."

Ragan clucked softly. "Shame. Can see there's been a lot of hard work put in on this place, but like I said, not easy for me to give you advice. Might help some if you'd go in, talk about it with your brother."

She frowned. "It would be a good idea. It's what I'd like to do if you think it won't upset him. He believes everything's been settled with Chandler."

"Put it to him that you'd like his opinion if Chandler comes back someday with the same old song."

She smiled briefly, turned down the hall for Pogue's room. Dan moved to the stove, felt the granite coffee pot. Still warm. Despite the heat a cup of coffee would taste good. Taking up a cup, he poured himself a measure of the strong, black liquid, swished it slowly about in the container.

If Ann Buckman decided to give in, sell the ranch to Chandler, then there was nothing to worry about. She would simply tell the rancher that some sort of a deal could be struck, and it would all be over and done with. If she decided to stick it out, fight. . . . He paused, considered that. He still had no choice but to take over, fort up the house, make preparations to hold out until the sheriff got there, just as he'd planned earlier.

And another day would slip by, another day that would put Jody Strickland that much nearer, if, indeed, he wasn't already in the Lagrima Valley, nosing about, asking questions, getting a line on him. He'd find the right answers, too. Any of Chandler's riders who had seen him would recognize the description, tell Jody right where the man he sought could be found. Maybe luck would be with him. Maybe the Mason City lawmen would arrive before Jody found his trail, and he could ride on. It could work out that way. . . .

He heard a sound behind him, came about. Ann, her face chalk white, drawn, her eyes closed, walked slowly into the room. Steadying herself with one hand placed on the table, she sank into a chair.

"Pogue's dead," she murmured in an empty voice.

XI

Ragan said nothing, and then after a bit turned, made his way down the hall to the bedroom. Stepping inside, he looked down at Buckman's stilled features. Death was no stranger to Dan Ragan; he had seen it in many forms, in many places, and was seldom moved, unless, as in this instance, it was a senseless thing that came to pass unnecessarily. Almost with anger, he reached across the bed, grasped the edge of the light, patch quilt, and drew it over Pogue's body. Wheeling, he backtracked to the kitchen. Ann lifted her face to him as he entered. She had herself well under control, only her eyes revealing the grief that wracked her.

"I was too late . . . we never got to talk," she said. "But I think I know what he would have wanted me to do."

"Hang onto the place."

She nodded. "He would have told me to do what I thought best, and safest for Earl and me. But down deep he'd be hoping we'd stay. This is the home he'd struggled so long and hard to make for us, and he'd feel we should keep it, regardless."

Regardless, Dan thought, *is just another word for big trouble.* But he did not voice it, said instead: "Means you'll have to fight Chandler."

"I know that," she replied in a weary voice. "And I won't ask you to stay, Dan. You have your own problems."

His expression did not change. "How you aiming to meet yours?"

"I'll simply face up to things as they come. I . . . I don't think Ross Chandler will harm me, being a woman, and I can. . . ."

Ragan's harsh laugh cut her words short. "You don't know a man like Chandler! Your being a woman makes no difference to him . . . only fixes it so's it's easier for him to do what he wants. Better get that straight in your head real fast."

Concern tugged at Ann Buckman's features. She got to her feet slowly. "Then I don't know . . . I'm not sure what I. . . ."

"You've got one way to go. Fort up, like we figured to do, and try to hold out until the law gets here."

"Fort up?"

Ragan stirred impatiently. So engrossed in worry over Pogue had she been that he had apparently failed to get through to her earlier.

"Yes. Get set to fight them off. Got to have guns waiting at every window. When Chandler and his outfit try to move in, we start shooting. If we can turn them back, hold them off until the sheriff and his deputies show up, then you've got a chance of hanging onto your ranch." Ragan paused, added in a voice somewhat tinged with scorn: "That is, if the sheriff's an honest man and don't lean toward Ross Chandler."

"But he's the law!"

"Wearing a badge don't make a man honest. He has to be that way, badge or not."

Ann gave him a hopeless look, settled heavily onto the chair again, a frail, frightened study of utter dejection.

"Then there's no use . . . no need. I don't know what to do. . . ."

"You said you'd fight," Ragan snapped, impatience sharpening his words. "That's what we'll do!"

"But if the sheriff won't help . . . ?"

"Don't know that he won't. Could be either way, and we'll not be able to tell until he's here."

"Then we could go through all this . . . fighting them off, I mean, maybe even getting shot . . . and then find out in the morning that he's on Chandler's side."

"About the way it adds up. Like everything else, you've got to gamble . . . play the odds. You believe you ought to hang onto your ranch, fight for it. Then, best thing you can do is figure the sheriff will be on the square. Got a hunch he is from what your brother said. Anyway, we'll risk it."

Frowning, she studied him. "Then you'll stay? Help?"

"Won't say I'm plumb happy about it, but I reckon I've got no choice. That boy, Earl, has got my horse, so I'll just have to wait around until he gets back."

Ann smiled in spite of herself, but as quickly she sobered. "What about that man trailing you? He'll hear. . . ."

"Just keep hoping he won't show up," Dan replied indifferently. "About all I can do. Could be the sheriff'll make it here before he does."

Abruptly he turned to the table where the weapons and supply of ammunition lay.

"We're going to be a mite short on guns," he said. "Got three, counting my Forty-Five. Best thing will be to put the rifle in the window of Earl's room, along with all the cartridges you have for it."

"Everything's here, on the table."

"Have to make them count. That scatter-gun had best be at your window. Riders coming in from that side'll be fairly close because of the brush. I'll take care of the yard with my pistol."

She thought that over, shook her head. "You won't be able to . . . not entirely, anyway . . . unless you go out onto the porch. The north side's hidden from in here."

"I'm aiming to keep them from ganging up on that side," he

explained. "You ever used a gun?"

Ann shook her head. "Back home there was no need, and it certainly wouldn't have been considered lady-like, especially for a schoolteacher. Out here, well, Pogue was going to teach me, for my own good, but we just never found the time."

"You'll learn today," Dan said brusquely. "I'll show you how to handle the rifle. Be the best for you, but first I got a little chore outside."

"Can I help?"

"Not with that. Have to get all the loose brush and weeds pulled back away from the house. Don't figure to make it easy for them to start a fire." He started toward the door, hesitated. "If you like, tote the rifle and the cartridges for it into Earl's room. Put them on a table or something close to the window where they'll be handy. Do the same with the shotgun and the shells for it."

She nodded her understanding and then, on impulse, laid her hands on his arm. "There could be somebody still out there, hiding in the brush. Please . . . be careful."

He grinned. "I'll watch sharp," he said, and moved out onto the porch. It was something to think about, he was forced to admit, and for the next few minutes he stood motionlessly at the end of the gallery, eyes probing the growth along the north and east sides of the yard where a man could find ample concealment.

He saw nothing to arouse suspicion and so set about clearing away anything near the house on all sides that could be put to a torch. It wasn't too much of a chore. Pogue, or perhaps it was the younger Earl, had kept the weeds at a respectable distance, and about all Dan had to concern himself with was the brush Chandler's riders had dragged in earlier.

That completed, he removed the dog that had been killed by one of the rancher's men, pulling it off into a small wash where he threw branches and rocks upon the lifeless form. There was nothing he could do about getting rid of the horse that had met a similar fate, since it would require a team in harness to pull the dead weight. And so he returned to the house.

Ann had placed the weapons as he had directed, and, after taking a survey from each window, he unloaded the rifle and showed the girl how to operate it. He had her spend a full fifteen minutes getting the hang of sighting along the barrel at chosen objects, pressing off the trigger, and then levering. Once the procedure was firmly established in her mind, he demonstrated how to refill the magazine.

"Reckon you're ready now," he said, propping the weapon on the table and against the window sill. "Time comes, aim at the man's middle, hold steady for a breath, and squeeze the trigger. You'll hit him."

A shudder passed through the girl. Dan Ragan reached out instantly, caught her wrist in a hard grasp.

"Don't be thinking that way," he snapped. "You keep remembering, if you don't shoot him first, he's going to shoot you."

Ann bit at her lower lip, dropped her head. "I'll remember."

Together they went back into the kitchen. Ragan poured himself another cup of coffee from the pot. It was stone cold but the bitterness had character and he relished it.

"I'll make some fresh," Ann suggested, moving near him. "I guess we ought to eat, too. A little, anyway."

He signified his agreement. Anything to keep her busy, her mind occupied, was a good idea. Chandler had said he would return at sundown. Figuring that he would likely cheat on that a little and move in earlier in hopes of seizing an advantage, they should still have grace for a couple of hours.

"Probably be a good idea for me to look after Pogue," Dan said, placing it as a gentle suggestion.

Instantly she whirled to him. "I don't want to bury him. Not until Earl gets back."

"Figured that," Dan said, setting his cup aside. "I was thinking about a coffin. Saw plenty of lumber in the barn. Be tools there, too. Be no trouble nailing one together."

"Of course," she murmured, turning back to the stove. "I'd appreciate it."

He started for the door, halted as a moment of caution came to him. "Don't figure we'll be bothered much for a couple of hours yet, but we'd best not bank on it. Be smart to take a look through Earl's window every now and then. When they come, they'll show there first."

"I'll watch," she answered.

Pogue Buckman kept an orderly workshop in one corner of the barn, Ragan discovered. A saw hung from a peg; there was a hammer, an adze, a hatchet, and a heavy, double-bitted axe for use at the woodpile. Nails were not so easily found, but eventually he located a gallon tin, its top cut out, half filled with the square-shouldered slivers of iron in various lengths.

There was plenty of two-inch planking, and, dragging up two sawhorses to serve as a working surface, Dan set himself to the task of constructing a tight box for the body of the elder Buckman. He worked at it steadily, pausing now and then to wipe the sweat from his brow, and deriving some satisfaction and relief from the pure physical labor being performed. He had just finished nailing the cross pieces to the lid when he saw Ann come through the door.

She was carrying a cup of coffee in one hand, had a lightweight blanket in the other. Silent, she halted beside the box, passed the coffee to him, and then hung the blue woolen cover on the edge of the coffin.

"I thought we could use this for a lining. It won't seem so bare, so cold."

Dan said—"Sure."—and leaned back against the wall, sipping at his cup.

Her hands traveled lightly over the sides of the box. "It's thick wood," she noted absently.

"Makes it pretty heavy. Couldn't find any thinner boards."

"I'm glad. Seems it should be that way . . . strong. Are you almost finished?"

"Just the lining, that's all."

"I can help with that."

"Fine. Won't take long."

"Then can we carry it into the house? It would be nice to have him in the parlor . . . sort of lie in state there. Nobody'll come to see him, I know, but us. But he was proud of that room even if we never got to use it much."

The coffin was exceptionally heavy because of the thick lumber, and would be difficult to handle for even two men. Dan's eyes fell upon a wheelbarrow tipped against a far wall; it offered the solution.

"Be no problem. I'll trundle it in. . . ."

His words ended as a quick rush of hoofs in the yard brought him up short. A gun crashed, sent echoes slamming through the recesses of the barn. Ross Chandler's exultant yell followed.

"You in there! Got you both cornered. Want to call it quits . . . and stay alive?"

XII

Ann's stricken face was turned to Ragan. "I . . . I shouldn't have left the house. I've let them slip in on us."

"It's all right," he said, glancing around the barn. There were windows in three sides, all high-placed and small. In the rear wall was another door.

"You hear?" Chandler's voice was hard, impatient. "I ain't going to waste no more time."

Dan eased nearer to the front, taking care not to place himself in a direct line with the doorway. When he reached a point where he could see most of the men, he halted. Chandler. Yates. Steve Denver. Three other riders he had never seen before—and one he had: Jim Korello. The dark, almost Indian-like killer had not changed, he noted.

At that moment two more cowpunchers came from the main house. They would have found Pogue's body; Ross Chandler would know shortly that he had only Ann Buckman and her young brother to deal with.

"What's your offer?" Ragan called.

Chandler's jaw sagged. He scrubbed at the stubble on his cheeks with a knotted fist, glanced around at his hired hands.

"Now don't that beat all!" he said with a laugh. "There they are, backed into a hole like a couple of old badgers, and he's wanting to know what I'm offering! Man's got the guts of an army mule!"

There was general laughter at the rancher's words. Only Korello saw no humor in them—or the situation. He continued to stare at the dark rectangle of the doorway, his eyes half shut, his features expressionless. When all was quiet again, he shifted on his saddle.

"Don't take no guts to stand behind a woman's skirts. And that's what he's doing."

From the shadowy interior of the barn Ragan considered the gunman with a cold smile. Korello knew him better than that—or at least he thought he did. It could be the man was just hoping to goad him into the open. And there was the possibility he'd heard rumors about Jody Strickland and how he had one of the West's top guns on the run.

"Well, he ain't against triggerin' a gun," Chandler said. "Got some boys shot up that prove that."

"You're talking about something else," Korello replied.

"Riding through the brush, dodging behind rocks and shooting is one thing. Anybody can do that. I'm talking about facing another man straight on . . . a showdown."

Dan scarcely heard. His eyes were on the two cowpunchers who had been inside the house. They were now reporting to Chandler. Abruptly the rancher looked up.

"You want to know what my deal is?" he shouted, smiling with satisfaction. "All right, I'll tell you."

Ragan turned to Ann, pointed to the door at the rear of the barn. "Where does that lead to?"

Her face was pale in the murky depths of the building, but her voice was steady, betrayed no fear. "There's a yard, a corral just outside. Back of that are the foothills."

He nodded. "Get down close to the door and wait for me."

The girl wheeled at once, hurried to the exit. Dan brought his attention back to the men in the yard. The pair who had visited the main house had remounted and joined the half circle. Nine men in all, now. Nine to one. Ragan grinned wryly. Nobody could ever say he got the best odds. It seemed he was always finding himself on the short end.

"Didn't get that!" he called. Chandler had been speaking during those moments when he was getting Ann set. He had no idea what the rancher had said, cared less, but it was necessary that he make it appear he was interested.

Ross Chandler cursed loudly. "Then open up your ears, god dammit! I ain't chewing this over again. Said I know Pogue Buckman's dead. Know the girl and that kid sure can't handle the place. So I'm telling them I'll take over."

"Just take over. . . ."

"Be paying them what I figure's right. Then I've got a little business with you, mister. Shooting up my crew way you did . . . I ain't standing for it. Brought along a friend of yours who aims to even up things for me."

"No friend of mine, and he knows it."

"That so? Ain't what he told me."

Korello had shifted again on his horse, but his small, sharp eyes never strayed from the barn's doorway.

"Come on out, Ragan," he said in a low voice. "Be good seeing you again. And maybe we can finish up that bit of business we had a couple or three years back."

Dan was silent for a long minute. He glanced over his shoulder at Ann. She was waiting beside the door. He must think first of her, and that left him no choice.

"I'd be a fool to step out there. Nine to one. Don't like that kind of odds."

"Oh, the rest of us'll pull off, get out of the way," Ross Chandler said. "This is betwixt you and Jim . . . and nobody else. He wants it that way. Told me he'd always had a hankering to have it out with you."

"That what you told him, Jim?"

"Sure did. Always sort of galled me way you strutted around, big like, too damn' good for everybody else. Told myself once that someday I'd blast that biggety out of you, cut you down to size. Figure that time's come."

"Something you ought to be sure of. Being dead's a mighty permanent thing. Mind telling me why you think you've got a chance now when you didn't back that other time?"

"Man gets older, slows down. And I hear tell you're running scared."

"So you're thinking your chances are good now."

"Always was good. Better'n that today. . . ."

"Well, what about it?" Chandler shouted angrily. "Seems to me you're both mighty long on talk . . . and I ain't about to just keep setting here while you jaw. Reckon you're a loser anyway, no matter how it goes."

"Was thinking just that," Ragan drawled, brushing at the

sweat clouding his eyes. He had been sparring for time, hoping to come up with an idea better than the solitary thought that had come to mind—flight. But there appeared to be no other answer.

"What's it going to be? I'm giving you about thirty seconds to make up your mind."

"All right. All right, but I got to talk to the lady."

"The hell . . . what about? She don't figure in this. I'll give her and the kid enough to get out of the country, and that's it. Then I'm burning this place to the ground."

"What about Pogue Buckman? Man deserves a decent burial."

"I'll see to it. All I'm interested in is getting this dump wiped out. Like a wedge in the middle of my range. Ain't natural."

"It was you who turned it into a wedge."

"God dammit! Quit arguing with me over nothing! I'm trying to treat you right, same as I did Buckman. You step out here, have this little duel with Jim. If he's good as he claims he is, it'll be good bye you. If he ain't and you top him . . . well, I'll make you a quick deal. You can ride on, scotfree."

"You're changing your mind mighty sudden."

"Just plain tired of all this yammering."

Chandler's promise would be about as reliable as quicksand, Dan thought, but it would be smart to play along.

"What about the lady?"

"Like I said, I'll look after her and the kid. No need for you to fret about it. Can't see as you got any call to go worrying about her, anyhow. You're going to be dead or else riding hell-for-leather out of the country."

"Guess you're right. One thing . . . how'll I know I'm going to get a fair shake when I step out there? You're all ringed in there, and every one of you ready to put a bullet in me."

"We'll pull back plenty far," Chandler said quickly, and

added: "You hear me, boys? Back off. We got to give them plenty of room."

Dan watched the slight confusion that followed, and then the milling horses and riders shaped up into a new line fifty feet or so away from the barn.

"That suit you, mister?" Chandler yelled mockingly.

"Some better," Dan answered, his eyes now on Jim Korello swinging lazily from his saddle and preparing to take up a stand at the end of the now cleared area fronting the structure.

"Then get the hell out here! We're waiting!"

"Take me a minute to tell the lady good bye. Reckon I won't be seeing her again, one way or another."

"Hurry it up, dammit!" the rancher shouted. "I . . . !"

Dan Ragan had already spun, was running as quietly and as fast as he could on a bad leg toward the rear of the barn where Ann waited. They'd not have much time to get outside, cross the open ground, and escape into the brushy hills. Ross Chandler's impatience was reaching a peak and his suspicions would mount with it. But it was their one chance and they had to make the best of it.

He reached the door, pushed it open. Ann hurried through into the small corral. Pointing to the gate in the opposite side, Ragan followed.

"Keep low and run," he said in a husky voice. "Got to lose ourselves . . . fast."

Ann made no reply, simply gave him an understanding look, and rushed on. Close on her heels, Ragan glanced over his shoulder. So far so good, but they'd barely started.

XIII

They broke from the corral and shortly reached the foot of the slope. Brush was thin here, no more than knee-high weeds, and the taller growth was another fifty yards distant. Running awkwardly on his injured leg, Ragan drew abreast Ann, caught her by the hand, and began to veer slightly left to where the ground was broken and uneven. There could be a ditch, a hollow—something that would afford them the protection he knew they could need very soon.

Ann gave him a desperate look. "I . . . can't run much . . . farther!" she gasped, stumbling over the rough terrain.

"Have to," he said in a tight voice, taking a firmer grip on her hand. "Got to reach those cedars before they get wise . . . if we can."

The small, clump-like trees would be only the first stop. A quarter mile beyond he could see the ragged face of a rocky, ledge formation. That would be their ultimate destination, a place where they could find hiding until help from Mason City arrived.

Suddenly Ann tripped. Ragan whirled to catch her, seeking to keep her from going down. He was partly successful as she went first to one knee, and then to the other. Hunched beside her, he gave her support as she fought to recover her breath.

"Go on . . . I can't run any more. . . ."

He shook the sweat from his eyes, glanced over his shoulder toward the barn. No one had appeared at the back door yet, an indication that Ross Chandler had not yet become convinced he'd been tricked. That was a bit of good luck, but he knew it wouldn't last long.

They were not far now from the cedars, but the bluff was still a considerable distance away. He looked around, searching for a hollow, a thick stand of weeds, a mound of earth—anything that would shield them from view. There were only the small, globular snakeweed plants, a few ragged ground swells—and little else.

Motion at the rear door of the barn caught his eye. Instantly, hunched beside the girl, he froze.

"Don't move," he warned.

A cowpuncher stepped out into the corral, glanced hurriedly about, and as quickly withdrew. The whole bunch would be swarming up the slope in a few minutes, Dan realized, and they had better not be there. Caught in the open as they were, they'd have no chance. Somehow they had to make it to the cedars, and then to the rock ledge.

Dan pulled himself partly upright. Grasping Ann by the arm, he got her onto her feet.

"I . . . can't," she protested weakly.

"You've got to," he said harshly. "In a couple of minutes more Chandler and his bunch will be coming around the side of the barn and heading up this hillside. They spot us, they'll have us cold."

He was already moving as he spoke, bent low, half dragging, half carrying the girl as he went. But his words had instilled a measure of strength in her; struggling yet to recover her breath, she fought to stay on her feet, to keep up with him.

The first of the deep, green cedars were just ahead and slightly above them on the steep slope. Not hesitating, Ragan changed course, angled upward toward them, knowing the sharper climb would slow the pace, but figuring the separating distance was much shorter.

He heard Ann gasp above the faint trickling sound of spilling gravel sliding out from under their feet. He tightened his grip upon her hand, conscious of the stabbing pain in his leg as greater strain was being placed upon it, continued on, literally dragging the girl with him until the first of the trees had been reached.

Collapsing behind the squat but thickly branched cedar, Ragan, heaving for wind, threw his attention to the barn. His throat tightened and a flare of alarm shot through him. Chandler and his hired hands had already circled the building, were hammering across the narrow space of ground that lay between the corral and the base of the slope.

Had the rancher and his men caught sight of them in those last, agonizing moments as they struggled to reach the trees?

"Are . . . we . . . safe . . . now?"

Ann Buckman's anxious question came with effort while she heaved for breath.

Ragan brushed at his jaw. "Starting to work the slope. Maybe they didn't see us. They'd come boiling straight up the hill for us if they had."

"Then we can stay here . . . rest . . . ?"

"Not for long. They'll comb us out with no trouble."

"Then what are we going to do?"

He twisted about, pointed to the frowning face of the butte. "If we can make it to there, odds are good we can lose them."

She studied the rough, upright formation outlining itself against the afternoon sky. "It's so far, and the slope looks so steep."

"Better to try and make it than just quit. Chandler's got a bullet waiting for both of us. He'd as soon use them right here on the slope as anywhere."

"Of course," she murmured, now breathing easier. "We'll have to try."

He grinned at her, glanced to the foot of the grade. Chandler had drawn his riders into a tight group. The rancher was pointing up the hillside, speaking and gesturing as he designated areas to be searched by different parties. He seemed to be directing the activities a bit farther south, probably because there was more brush in evidence in that particular section. He hadn't noticed that when he and the girl had come from the corral, Dan realized—he was now pleased that he had not.

He looked to the ledge, scanned the sloping land below it. "Be a hard climb, sure enough, but there's plenty of cover we can use. Got a hunch that's an arroyo there to the left, too. We can work our way up it maybe."

Drawing himself to a crouch, he placed his attention once more on Chandler and his men. They were fanning out, beginning to search the hillside. The rider headed more or less in their direction was an older man astride a small buckskin. He was slumped in the saddle, appeared worn and tired. Likely he had spent the previous night on herd duty, and then had been drafted into use by the rancher without any rest.

"Stay close to me," Ragan said, moving out from behind the twisted, wind-whipped little tree.

Angling cross the face of the grade, working from clump to clump in order to prevent their being seen by the men below, he pointed for what he took to be a narrow wash that came down from the butte. Halfway a fairly good roll in the land cut them off from any possible notice by Chandler's crew, and under cover of this new and unexpected protection they were able to quicken their pace and gain the arroyo.

It was not as deep as Dan had hoped for, but it was some below the general level of the land, and it did run on a more or less straight line for the ledges.

He halted in the narrow, trench-like drain, supporting the girl while she again fought to recover her spent breath, and then, as her breast gradually ceased its convulsive heaving, he took her hand once more and pressed on. It was no longer necessary to walk in a crouching position as the arroyo was bordered along most of its erratic course with clumps of rabbit brush, oak, mountain mahogany, and other growth.

They moved on steadily, unable to see what was happening below, knowing only that Chandler and his riders were searching, that eventually they would find their way to the arroyo. But with luck, Dan figured, he and the girl would by then have reached the rocky area of the butte and found a suitable place in which to hide.

The sharp, hard *click* of metal against stone brought them to a sudden halt. Ragan dropped to his knees, pulled Ann down beside him. A horse was somewhere below them—and not far.

Hunched on the sandy floor of the wash, they watched, waited. The *thud* of the horse's hoofs grew louder, nearer. Dan realized in the next moment that the rider was coming up the arroyo, either following their tracks, or working on a hunch that suggested the pair for whom he searched had taken such a route.

Desperate, Ragan glanced around. The wash made a slight bend to the left a few steps farther on. Touching Ann by the arm, he crawled that short distance and there, on the far side of the curve, drew back hard against the inside wall with the girl pressed closely behind him.

The horse's shoe *clicked* metallically again, this time only strides away. The *thump* of his hoofs seemed almost on top of them, and abruptly the rider was there before them—the old man on the buckskin.

He saw Ragan in the same instant Dan lunged to his feet, pistol held as a club in his hand. Surprise and fear blanched his weathered features as the heavy .45 thudded into the side of his head. A groan slipped from his lips as he sagged to one side, fell to the ground.

Downslope a voice carried across the hot hush. "Amos? Hey, Amos . . . that you up there?"

Ragan bent over the fallen man, straightened slowly. The others were nearer than he had figured.

"Amos?"

"Right here," Dan shouted, muffling his voice. "Keep going."

He didn't know if he'd get away with it or not; he could only hope. Wheeling, he grabbed Ann by the hand, started up the arroyo at a fast walk.

"Got to get out of here . . . fast," he said tautly.

XIV

"Amos!"

The shout came again from the lower part of the slope, this time the tone sharp and suspicious. Scrambling up the arroyo, fighting to stay on his feet while he ignored the pain in his leg, holding tightly to Ann, Ragan swore softly.

He hadn't fooled the man below when he'd answered. In a short time he could expect him—possibly others—to locate the wash, hurriedly follow out its course. They'd find the old man, lying on the sand, know instantly what had happened. The alarm would be raised, and in no time at all the area would be crawling with Chandler's men.

Ann went to her knees, a sob bursting from her lips as she strained for breath. He dragged her upright, looked ahead. The butte was only a dozen strides away. He could see the cleavage where the arroyo gashed its face, twisted on upward to gain the rim.

"Hey, up here!"

The rider had found Amos. Ragan swore again and, pivoting, thrust his arms under Ann, lifted her bodily off her feet, and staggered the remaining distance to the rocks.

"Over this way! He's gone and caught old Amos! Maybe killed him!"

The cowpuncher was shouting his information as Dan reached the mouth of the wash, halted, lowered Ann to the ground. He was trembling from the effort; his leg screamed with pain and his body was soaked in sweat. Resting himself against the rocks, he pointed into the arroyo, narrower here than on the slope below.

"Keep going . . . climb," he managed.

Nodding woodenly, Ann moved into the opening. At once he came about, began to catch up the wind-blown weeds and litter scattered around the foot of the butte. Ann paused, frowning, and then, when she saw him drawing it into the mouth of the gully, she turned and began to claw her way up the narrow, cluttered defile. But her strength was gone and she had never fully recovered her breath. Halting again, she sank back against the flat side of a massive outthrust of granite, able only to wait.

He had pulled several clumps of dry brush up into the entrance to the arroyo. He had brushed away the prints they had made at the foot of the butte, although the loose shale and gravel made such precautions more or less unnecessary. Pausing to glance over what he had accomplished, he reached down, picked up several of the weed clumps, and began backing up the trail, dragging the dry, crackling growth with him.

Releasing the clumps after he was well inside the wash, he continued on until he reached Ann. The entrance was well blocked and to a casual observer the pile of weeds jammed in the mouth of the arroyo would indicate the wash had not been cleared for months.

He glanced at the girl, brushed at the sweat on his face. She was rested, was breathing normally at last. Dust and dirt streaked her cheeks and her arms, and her clothing was torn from the numerous falls taken. But seeing him looking at her, she produced a faint smile.

"I must look a sight."

He grinned, amused that her first concern was for appearance while a dozen armed men, at that exact moment, were prowling the hillside below, ready to kill them both at the first opportunity.

And they were working upgrade. He could hear their voices, the occasional *crash* of brush, the *clatter* of displaced rock.

"Expect we'd best keep going," he said, moving past her and reaching back for her hand. "Somebody'll likely remember that a trail goes up this wash. Weeds may stop them . . . maybe not."

Ann glanced up the twisting, ragged channel. "Do we have to

climb all the way to the top? I'm not sure I. . . ."

"We go until we find a place to hide," he cut in. "Could be part way . . . could be on the top. Once we're there, we can lay low till dark."

She drew herself to her feet and stepped in close behind him. He took her hand, placed it on the center rear of his thick, leather belt, hooked her fingers over it.

"Hang on tight," he said, starting the ascent. "It'll help some."

They made their way slowly, cautiously, and as quietly as possible on the steep declivity. Sounds of spilling gravel, the crackling of brush or the thud of falling rock would carry far in the late afternoon's hush, and he was endeavoring to avoid any such disturbance.

Once they reached a good place of concealment, their problems would be over for the time being. All they'd need do was wait it out until Earl Buckman returned with the law. That realization caught at him, lodged in his mind. The sheriff and those with him would be taken to the ranch by the boy; they would find no one there. There was but one answer to that. He would have to return to the Buckman place, be there when McGaffey and his deputies arrived, otherwise the lawman would find nothing to warrant his taking action. And he'd not listen to charges made by a boy, not even when the body of a dead man lay in the bedroom of the house could be claimed as proof. A man could die from a bullet for many reasons and causes, and his own testimony—that of a drifter—would go unheeded. No, his first thought—of leaving Ann safely hidden on the butte while he made the dangerous trip back to the ranch—would have to be forgotten. It would be necessary for her to be there. Only her charges would count with Sheriff McGaffey—if, indeed, anyone's would.

So far they'd had fair luck, almost good; if it continued to run with them, they could manage all right. They'd simply wait until dark, until things quieted down, and then make their way back to the ranch. It would be a touchy situation; he was not fooling himself that, come dark, Chandler would call off his wolves and withdraw.

It would be just the opposite. Ross Chandler had committed himself to violence in its worst form now, and it would be necessary to complete what he had begun in order to cover up all evidence of his crime. That meant wiping out the Buckmans entirely, along with anyone who had stood by them. As far as his own men went, he had no problem there; they'd remain loyal to him partly because they worked for him, took money in payment for what they were ordered to do, and partly because it would be unsafe to do otherwise.

Chandler would have it all his own way unless Ann Buckman, with the confirming support of both Earl and himself, was there to accuse the rancher and make her charges to the lawman. It would all take Chandler unawares; he did not know McGaffey had been sent for, and. . . .

"Wait . . . please, Dan. . . ."

At the girl's plea Ragan halted short. He'd been so lost in his train of thought that he'd climbed steadily, giving no consideration to the ordeal he was undoubtedly putting her through.

He allowed her to settle back against the rim of the arroyo, half sitting, half standing but resting, nevertheless. "Sorry," he murmured ashamedly. "Reckon I forgot how hard this is on you."

She brushed wearily at her eyes. "I'll be all right in a minute." Glancing up the trail, she added: "Is it much farther to the crest?"

"Not sure. Never been here, but I don't see how it can be."

Turning, he climbed out of the wash, and using care, dodging from one brush clump to another, he made his way forward to a point where he could see the slope below, the jagged rim of the butte above.

Four riders were in sight halfway up the grade. They were angling across the face of the hillside in a skirmish line, but they appeared to be traveling for some specific point rather than searching—and they were heading north. Two more were climbing the arroyo, their goal doubtless the base of the bluff. Six men. Where were the others? Where was Ross Chandler? He did not appear to be among those visible. Nor was Jim Korello. At least none of those Dan could distinguish seemed to be the gunman. Something was. . . .

Motion well down on the flat below drew his attention. Another group of riders—a half a dozen at least—and all heading back to the Buckman place. Chandler would be one of the party, that was certain. Why would he be pulling out? It was still a good two hours until full dark, and he wouldn't be turning back unless he was certain of his ground.

The four men riding north. . . . It cleared abruptly for Dan Ragan. Those riders had been dispatched to circle the bluff, come in from the top of the formation; two others were working their way up the only alternate trail. Chandler had them trapped in between, was convinced of it—so sure of it in fact that he was taking part of the crew and returning to the Buckman ranch where he would likely proceed with his plan to burn the buildings to their foundations.

And there was no one to prevent it. Pogue was dead; Ann was driven into hiding and soon to be reckoned with along with the one man who had befriended her; the kid, as the rancher termed Earl, nowhere to be found, and of no consequence anyway. All had panned out just as Chandler liked.

Grim, Ragan made his way back to the gully, dropped down beside the girl. "Rim's not much farther," he said, deciding to tell her nothing of what he had seen and concluded. "Be a place there where we can rest."

"Is Ross Chandler and the others still out there?"

Ragan nodded. "Hunting us . . . like we were a couple of rabbits. Up to us to find ourselves a good hole."

"Do you think they'll find our trail?"

He shrugged. "They know the country." He was still unwilling to tell her what he thought was the truth, that Chandler's men were closing in from two sides, hoping to trap them in between, that Chandler himself had. . . .

"I'm ready." She broke into his thoughts, got to her feet.

He gave her a moment to get her fingers locked again about his belt, and then resumed the climb. The crest of the butte was in sight, but what they would find there he was not certain, having had only a glimpse from the slope. It would take a cave that could be well masked, a gash in the rocky surface that might be covered over, a wide expanse of thick brush.

"There it is, right ahead of us," Ann said suddenly, relief in her voice. "I . . . I thought we'd never make it."

XV

On hands and knees they crawled out of the wash, no more than a slight depression here at its source, and sprawled full-length at the edge of the butte's plateau-like summit.

"Got to pull back from the rim," Dan said. "No sense letting them spot us."

He began to crawl toward the inner side of the plateau where they could rise and not be silhouetted against the darkening sky. The girl followed obediently. Gaining a point sufficiently back from the rim, he rose, helped her to her feet.

"Wait here," he said, and once more dropped flat on his belly.

He returned to the lip of the butte, but this time working his way to the side overlooking the broader north slope. There was no sign of the four riders; apparently they had begun their climb to the crest, were hidden from him by intervening rolls of land

and clumps of cedars. He had no idea how much time it would require for them to gain the plateau from that angle but guessed that he and Ann had a few minutes left in which to get set.

Dropping back to the girl, he took her again by the hand and, sizing up the area with a swift, probing glance, picked his way over the loose shale and through the thin scattering of bushes to a fairly large mound of earth and rock 100 yards or so back from the rim.

Climbing to its top, he found he could watch the mouth of the trail as well as the upper end of the plateau from the slight depression in its center. The small crater-like area was filled with dead leaves and other litter, had evidently served as a lair for wild animals. By rearranging some of the smaller boulders strewn about, it could be converted into an effective hiding place and fortress, should it come down to gunfire.

"What we're looking for," he said, again throwing a glance to the north. "Find yourself a place to sit . . . there in the bottom . . . while I do a bit of fixing up."

Ann sank gratefully onto a flat rock, sighing deeply. Ragan began at once to move in the boulders scattered on the slight slope, tumbling the larger ones end over end, tossing in those of a smaller size.

When he had what he judged to be a sufficient amount, he stepped down into the depression, set to work arranging the stones, building a circular wall of irregularly placed rocks around the edge of the crater. That done, he brushed away all evidence of activity with a leafy branch torn from an oak shrub, and then took his place beside the girl.

"Not much like home." He grinned, once more checking the north edge of the plateau and the mouth of the arroyo where the trail ended. "But it'll do, if trouble starts."

"Like a fort," she murmured, looking around. "We ought to be safe here."

They settled down to await the coming of night—and whatever it might bring. Ann was pretty much in dead center of the stone-rimmed pit, Ragan leaning against the forward edge where he could keep all the ground before them under close watch.

"Dan," she said suddenly, impulsively reaching for his arm. "Isn't that smoke down in the valley?"

He swung his attention to the streamers twisting into the sky. While he watched, the wisps grew thicker, darker. He'd been right about Chandler.

"Your place," he said quietly, an angry edge to his voice. "They're burning it down."

The loss seemed not to disturb her greatly; her thoughts were for her dead brother. "Pogue . . . his body was in the house!"

He continued to study the smoke, settling now into a black, ugly cloud hanging low over the land. "Expect they gave him a burying. Coffin was all ready."

Such was not likely, he knew, but to let her feel otherwise relieved her anxiety. Ross Chandler would waste no time or energy on what he deemed an unnecessary task.

She settled back slowly. "The house . . . ranch wasn't much . . . but it was ours . . . and all we own is there. I don't know how . . . where we'll begin."

"Still got the land," Ragan said, eyes shifting to the brush at the mouth of the trail. "That's what counts. Can always build another house."

"We may not even have that," she replied listlessly.

"The law's got a few teeth. Chandler can't lay claim to your range unless you sell it to him, or. . . ."

She frowned, looked closely at him as he paused. "Or what?"

"What I'm meaning," he said hesitantly, "is that he'd have to have a deed. . . ."

"No, what you meant was that the only other way he could

get the land, if I refuse to sell, would be to kill us, Earl and me. That's what you meant."

Ragan made no reply.

The girl smiled ruefully. "I'm not afraid to hear that, or to know that it's what I'm facing. Pogue's already dead because of that terrible man, and maybe Earl and I will be, too, but don't think I'm fooling myself. I've grown up a lot in the last twelve hours."

"Know you have. Took a lot of sand to hold up under what you have."

"And it will get even worse, won't it?"

In this he figured it was best not to lie, but to make her fully aware of their problems and possibilities.

"You can bet on it. Thing we've got to do is stay alive until morning, give that sheriff time to get here."

"You're thinking of those men, following us up the trail in the wash . . . ?"

"And four more Chandler sent around the north end of the butte to come down on us from above . . . box us in."

"I . . . I didn't know about them."

"We're pretty well hid, and it'll be dark soon, probably before they can get here."

"And your plan is to just stay here? Wait?"

He nodded. "Leastwise until near morning. Figure then, that while it's still dark, we ought to head back down the trail and make it to the ranch. Got to be there when the law rides in. Be up to you to talk to this McGaffey, make your charges to him against Chandler."

"Charges?"

"Sure. He's guilty of murder, same as he's guilty of burning down your ranch, your property. If that sheriff's on the square, you'll have Chandler nailed down tight once and for all."

"It wasn't Chandler who shot Pogue. It was one of his men,

but I don't know which."

"Chandler sent him to do it, and that's enough to put him away for a good many years if not to hang him."

Ann settled back, her shoulders going down, her eyes closing. She had managed, somehow, with the bit of handkerchief she carried, to clean the dust and dirt streaks from her skin, but there was nothing she could do about the tears in her dress.

"It all seems like a nightmare!" she said in a worn voice. "When we were still home, waiting for Pogue to send for us, we'd sometimes get letters from him telling us about the trouble he was having. I never really thought much of it . . . certainly I never dreamed it could be this way. It's like there was no civilization out here at all. Only a cruel savage world where just the ruthless people can stay alive."

"It's a hard life, got to admit that," Ragan said. "And a man . . . or a woman . . . has to be strong to lick it. They don't have to be the way you say . . . ruthless. Sure, you have that kind . . . the Chandlers . . . but you have them back there in what you call civilization, too. Thing is they're not out in the open where you can see them. What's the difference in a man shutting down on a mortgage, taking everything from some widow or somebody that's sick and unable to help himself, and the way a man like Ross Chandler does things?"

"They don't use a gun . . . kill . . . like he did Pogue."

"There are other ways to kill a man besides a bullet . . . break his spirit, his will, his need to live. . . ."

"I know," she murmured with a slight shrug of her shoulders. "Only it seems different. Out here a person is so alone! Dan, I don't know what I would have done if you hadn't come along."

He gave her a brief smile. "You would have made out. Folks have a habit of facing up to what they must when the time comes. They just never know for sure they can until the moment's right there in front of them."

"Maybe. Earl and I . . . we both were so helpless against those men. And with Pogue wounded, everything looked so hopeless. I'll always be grateful to you."

Ragan's glance was on the valley where now the streamers and clouds of smoke had fused, become an ugly, gray-black pall hanging over the area of the Buckman ranch. Chandler's bunch would have made a thorough job of it; there'd be nothing left standing. He shifted his attention to the north, the girl's words bringing something else to mind—Jody Strickland. Jody would come from that direction, too.

He had thought little about Jody, his mind being so occupied with Ann Buckman's problems and the need to see her safely through her ordeal. But Jody wouldn't have forgotten him; either he was already in the Lagrima Valley, or else very close.

"That man who's following you . . . is he who you're thinking about now?"

A trace of surprise crossed his face at her question. "It shows that plain?"

Ann nodded. "A sort of strange look comes into your eyes, a kind of sadness, I guess it is. You never did tell me about it. Once you started to and then something came up. There was a woman, I think you said."

Ragan stared unseeingly at the sky beyond the edge of the butte. It was darkening steadily now as the sun at last had slid behind the ragged horizon in the west.

"Yeah, there was a woman. Clare, her name was. Was a time when we meant a lot to each other, the days when I was working cows for Jess Ungalls up Wyoming way. She was the daughter of a neighboring rancher. Then Jody's pa came into the picture. He'd lost his wife a few years back, and, when he met Clare, he decided she was what he wanted. Colby Strickland was a mighty fine-looking man, with high-toned manners and plenty of money. Could see I didn't stand a show against him, so I backed off, told Clare I'd keep out of her way, that the choice was hers. Ended up she picked Strickland."

"And you moved on?"

"The day they got married. I stuck around long enough to see them come out of the church, his boy Jody . . . he was about fifteen or sixteen then . . . with them. That told me Clare was all set, so I cleared out."

Ann was frowning. "Then how did you happen to get mixed up with them again?"

"Was riding through a town one day, stopped for a drink in a saloon, and there Strickland was. Found out then he was a gambler . . . always had been . . . and a crooked one from what I overheard. He didn't look like much, pretty well down on his luck, it was easy to see. Besides that, the bottle had got the best of him. Figured I'd look up Clare and see if there was anything I could do. Found out where they were living . . . a little shack at the edge of town. Rode out that same morning and the woman I saw I'd never have guessed was her if she hadn't told me. She was thin as a rail, had a bad cough . . . and there were dark bruises on the side of her face.

"I sort of flew off the handle when I saw her and was all for going back to the saloon and bringing Colby Strickland to account. She wouldn't hear of it. Things hadn't turned out the way she'd figured, but it was her bargain and she said she'd live with it. We sort of talked about everything then. I found out his boy Jody hadn't been around for a couple of years but was working on a ranch not too far off. Hardly ever saw him, she said, but that he did come in once in a while to see his pa. Seemed to think a lot of him.

"Later, back in town, I got to stewing it around in my head, and then decided that I'd best ride on since Clare wouldn't let me do anything about her problem, and I was afraid, if I saw much of Strickland, I'd lose my head and do something about it. Did figure it would be a good idea to drop back, leave an address with Clare where she could get word to me in case there was ever a need."

"That's when the trouble started . . . ?"

"It was. I rode up to the shack. First thing I heard was Clare crying. I went in fast, found him beating her. Kept accusing her of seeing me on the sly, and a lot of fool stuff like that. I jerked him off, threw him up against the wall. Turned then to pick Clare up. She was hurt, needed a doctor, I could see that. About the time I leaned over her, she screamed. From the corner of my eye I saw Strickland coming up with his sleeve gun. I drew and fired. Got him dead center but his bullet . . . his bullet hit Clare. She died a few minutes later, me holding her."

"Oh, no!" Ann cried softly in a shocked voice.

"I rode in, got the town marshal, took him and some others back to the shack. Told him what had happened. The marshal said he'd been expecting something like this. Strickland was a mean one, he said, along with being a cardsharp and a swindler. Was about two jumps away from getting himself run out of town. The marshal cleared me of any blame. Guess it was easy to see how it had all come about, so I saw to it that they both got buried decent and asked the marshal if he'd explain to Jody when he saw him, tell him I was sorry things had worked out the way they did . . . and moved on."

"Then why is he following you? The law didn't hold you at fault for the shooting."

"Seems he just wouldn't believe what the marshal told him. And, of course, he remembered me from the past, and that Clare and I had once been pretty close and that his pa had taken her away from me. Guess he added things like that in his mind and came up with an answer that said I killed them both because of what they'd done. Set out right then to find me, put a bullet in my head."

"And you've been trying to avoid him ever since."

"Kept me on the move," Ragan admitted heavily. "I'm hoping to shake him one of these days, maybe in Mexico. Sure hope the time never comes when I'm forced to fight him."

"I hope for that, too, for both our sakes," Ann said. "And I hope and pray that stopping to help me like you have won't bring the meeting about. I'd feel it was all my fault."

"We ever throw down on each other, there won't be anybody special at fault. It'll be that it just happened."

Dan lowered his gaze from the darkening sky to the now deeply shadowed land, let it drift on to the north edge of the plateau. No sign of Chandler's riders. That was good. They'd not arrive before night closed in. He brought his eyes then to the opposite side of the area, to the mouth of the trail, and stiffened perceptibly. The change in him did not escape Ann.

"What is it?" she asked in a low whisper.

"Something moved out there," he replied, reaching for his pistol.

XVI

Abruptly the dark shape of a man stood, soft-edged, against the background of the sky. A moment later another figure emerged from the shallow mouth of the arroyo, took up a stance beside the first.

"We'll play hell rousting them out now . . . dark as it is," one said in a tone of disgust. "We ain't even for certain they're up here."

"They're here. Ain't no doubt in my mind."

Jim Korello's voice. The gunman hadn't been with Chandler and those who returned to burn down the Buckman place, after all; he'd been left in charge of the group designated to continue the hunt—bring it to a successful conclusion. It was a fitting job for a killer, Ragan thought.

"Listen, you hear something?" It was Korello again. Dan's grip tightened upon his revolver. He would avoid shooting if at all possible, not wanting to give away their position to any other Chandler men in the vicinity, but if Korello and the cowpuncher with him became suspicious of the rocky mound, came in close to investigate, he'd be left with no choice.

"There! Heard it again!"

Ragan had caught the sound that time. It had come from the far side of the little mesa crowning the butte. He watched both men drop to a crouch. Pale light glinted upon the weapons held ready in their hands.

"Aw, god dammit! It's only Gates and the others," the man with Korello said, straightening up. "Hey, Buster, we're over here!"

Four riders broke from the shadows at the edge of the plateau, made their way across to the mouth of the trail.

"Plumb happy you hollered, Toby," the cowpuncher in the lead observed as they drew to a stop. "The two of you standing there had us all thinking for a minute we'd caught up with that pair."

Korello spat. "You going blind, Gates? One of us look like a woman to you?"

"Was the trouble . . . just couldn't tell."

Silence dropped over the party. Somewhere in the distance a cougar split the night with its chilling screech. Leather creaked as a man shifted on his saddle.

A voice said: "No signs of them, eh?"

Toby yawned, stretched. "Nothing. Not a dang' thing. Figured for sure they'd come up the wash . . . leastwise Chandler and Jim here did. Too dark for tracking, and we didn't kick them out of the brush nowheres."

"You look around up here?" Gates asked, swinging his horse about.

"Just got here. But reckon you can see same as us, there ain't no place for hiding. They'd've kept running, was they in front of us, and you'd 'a' bumped into them on the other trail."

"We didn't. I'm a-guaranteeing they didn't come that way. Seen some smoke back in the woods . . . campfire. Whoever it was took off before we could get there."

"Indians, likely. That drifter and the woman wouldn't have stopped to build no fire."

"What we figured," Gates said, "so we didn't waste no time hunting around. What's on west of here?"

Toby took a half a dozen steps deeper into the clearing. Ragan dropped his hand on Ann's arm, pressed it reassuringly. She was trembling from fear or cold, he could not be sure which.

"Another bluff, higher'n this one. Can't get up it from the front. Got to go clean around to the west side."

"Wouldn't have headed that way then."

"Not if one of them knows the country, which the woman don't, being a greenhorn. That jasper with her . . . I ain't so sure about him."

Gates said: "Well, best we be sure. Couple of us'll circle back toward there, have a look."

"You ain't apt to spot them in the dark!"

"Can try," Gates said, then, leaning over, peered into the older man's face. "You want to tell Ross Chandler you didn't figure it was worth the trouble having a look everywhere after them orders he give us?"

Toby thrust his hands into his back pockets, wagged his head. "Nope, ain't about to do that. But the way I see it, not even a hoot owl could find anything out there, dark as it is."

"Won't argue with that, but I know better'n to do any belly-aching about it. What're you two aiming to do next?"

Korello, who had remained silent during the conversation, said: "Head back down to the flat. Not much else we can do.

And Ross said we was all to meet at the Buckman place in the morning . . . report in."

"Be smart for one of you to stake out somewheres along that trail . . . maybe at the bottom . . . just in case they give us all the slip?"

"What I had in mind," Korello said stiffly. "You look after your end of it, I'll see to mine. Where'll you be?"

"I'm taking Lasater and swinging in toward that other bluff Toby was talking about. George and Carl'll go back the same way we come up, just to be sure we didn't override them. Meet down on the flat."

Korello was staring directly at the mound of rocks, apparently wondering if the mass was worth investigating. From where the gunman and the others stood, Dan realized the formation would appear to be no more than a slight rise in the earth almost devoid of weeds and other growth. He hoped Korello would accept it as such. Against six men with only his pistol. . . .

"Better ride easy," Korello said, his tone again drawling and friendly. "Walk your horses quiet and keep both eyes peeled. I know this Ragan. Corner him and he'll kill you sure . . . unless you can nail him first. Come on, Toby, let's head back. I'm starting to think like you . . . that they never come this way in the first place."

Abruptly the gunman and his partner turned into the trail. Gates and the men with him kneed their horses about, again faced the north.

"You heard what Jim said . . . keep your eyes open now. Go blundering into this bird and you'll end up dead."

"He's going to have the best of it," one of the riders said. "We'll be a-setting high up on these saddles, showing big as a barn, and with the racket these jugheads'll be kicking up. . . ."

"You come to a place where you think he might be hiding,

smart thing'll be to pile off and walk," Gates cut in. "Try thinking ahead a bit, George. Could do you some good."

The rider shrugged. "Maybe so, but sure seems like a lot of wasted time. Be smarter, I'm thinking, to pull off, wait for daylight. Then a man could see what he was doing. Besides, I'm mighty hungry. Ain't et since breakfast."

"Neither's the rest of us," Gates snapped. "Now, you got any more bellyaching to do before we head out? Let's get it off your chest."

"I ain't exactly griping," the man paired with George said, "but is it going to be all right if we head for the ranch when we get to the bottom? I'm agreeing with George . . . this hunting in the dark is danged foolish. And like him, I'm sure hungry."

Gates heaved a long sigh. "Tell you what. I don't give a good god damn what you do when you get to the bottom! Quit. Run a foot race. Take a flying jump at the moon. All the same to me because it'll be you explaining to Chandler when you're done. Me 'n' Lasater's going to have a look-see, best we can, at that other bluff and the country around it. Then I can tell the boss that we hunted for the pair like he said he wanted us to . . . and not back off when we say it. And just could be we'll find them. Hate for that to happen and not be the ones who dug them out. You think you'd hanker to explain something like that to him, George?"

After a long moment George said: "Nope, reckon not. Come on, Carl, let's get to this here looking."

"Just go careful," Gates said, his tone losing its edge. "And George, when you pass that pile of rocks, have yourself a gander at it up close. Don't see how a man could hide himself there, but you look just the same."

XVII

Ragan drew back. Reaching for the girl, he pulled her to him, covered her body with his own, thus masking the lighter color of her dress. Gun in hand, he watched the man called George swing away from his companions, angle for the mound of rocks.

Farther on, Gates and Lasater were moving into the night, becoming only vague blurs. Korello and his partner, Toby, apparently were well on their way down the arroyo trail as there were no sounds coming from that direction.

Dan felt Ann trembling against him as tension built with the slowly passing moments. He wished he could say something to her, whisper a word that would calm her fears—even just touch her hand. But he knew to move or make the slightest sound could prove disastrous.

The muted *tunk-a-tunk* of the approaching horse became louder. Head down, Ragan could not see, could only judge the position of Chandler's man by sound. He heard George hawk, spit. The saddle *creaked,* an iron shoe *clicked* against stone. The hoof *thumps* became loud—so close Dan thought that the man was riding into the rocky craters. And then the *thuds* ceased.

"Well, I'll be god damned," George muttered in a startled voice.

Ragan came out of the pit in a swift lunge, hurling himself at the cowpuncher with a deadly accuracy of a cat springing upon its prey. He lashed out with his pistol, hoping for a lucky strike, felt a surge of satisfaction as the weapon connected somewhere on George's head. The rider groaned, began to spill from the saddle while Dan, hanging on, fought to keep clear of the hoofs of the shying horse.

George struck the ground with solid force. The horse, free of its burden, pulled back, halted, obedient to the trailing reins. Ragan shot a glance at the cowpuncher's companion, Carl. The rider was still moving off through the murky night, holding his mount to a tired walk as he waited for George to rejoin him. He'd get suspicious soon, wonder what was causing the delay.

Ragan wheeled to Ann. "Come on," he said in a hoarse whisper.

She came out of the pit instantly. He crossed to the waiting horse, stepped to the saddle, and then, reaching down, caught the girl by the hand and swung her up behind him.

"Keep close," he said. "Got to make that Carl think I'm his partner. He gets a look at your dress. . . ."

He felt her shift, draw herself up tightly against him, make some sort of adjustment with her clothing. She had gathered in the garment, he guessed, was leaving little of it not hidden by his bulk.

"How can we get by him?" she wondered in a small voice.

"Aim to stall much as I can, like I was doing a good job of looking. Soon as we reach some thick brush or trees, we'll lose him. Ready?"

"Ready," she murmured.

Roweling the horse lightly, Dan moved away from the mound of rocks, keeping the horse pointed directly at Carl, now a short 100 yards or so along and barely visible in the pale light. The rider had not slowed or looked back as yet. Ragan wished then he'd taken time to make certain George didn't rouse for a few more minutes, but he'd been afraid to press his luck, had felt it best to follow as quickly as possible.

"Nothing?"

Carl's question, reaching through the quiet to him, brought him up sharply.

"Nothing," he replied, mimicking George's voice as well as he could. Unlike a similar occasion earlier, when he attempted to parrot the rider called Amos, he had heard George speak and was able to provide a passable imitation.

He remained well back, was endeavoring to make it appear

he was searching the low brush and scrub cedars and junipers scattered along the plateau. Noting this, Carl swung farther to his right, began a desultory probing of growth on his side of the little mesa.

"We ain't finding them up here!" he called irritably. "I misdoubt they ever come . . . like Toby and Jim said."

"Maybe you're right," Ragan answered, keeping his response to a minimum of words.

Anxious, he looked ahead. They should be getting into an area where cover would be available and an escape could be effected. A few moments later he saw where the plateau broke off, began the lengthy decline to the flat below. The solid darkness of thickly growing trees, pines and other large varieties, made the slope appear to be a black void. Once they reached there. . . .

"Somebody's got a fire going down there!" Carl shouted suddenly.

Ragan did not halt. Carl, however, had pulled up to the edge of the bluff, stopped.

"Come, take a look. See if you can make out who it is."

Dan Ragan gauged the distance to the first of the pines. Too far. They'd never make it without Carl realizing who they were, and open up with his gun. And even if he missed, the shots would bring the rest of Chandler's men in a hurry. Gates and Lasater were probably no more than a mile or two on west.

"That'll be Korello . . . and Toby," he said, pausing. "Them two we're hunting wouldn't be building a fire."

Carl remained motionless for a time, then moved on. "Just about who it is. And if I know that Toby, he's got a bottle that they're a-passing back and forth."

Dan Ragan felt the girl's arms, locked around his middle, slack off as relief poured through her. "Not much farther," he said in a low voice. "We get to those trees ahead, we'll be in the clear."

He cast a glance at Carl. The cowpuncher was allowing his horse to amble on slowly, pick his way along the trail near the rim of the butte. Dozing, Dan guessed. They would have no problem slipping away from him.

The first of the pines were immediately ahead. A moment later Ragan saw that the path along the edge of the butte apparently veered inward, and that Carl's mount, following it, would bring them to a side-by-side position shortly.

At once he cut left, guiding his own horse into a thicket of mountain mahogany and other low brush, thereby abandoning the main trail. The rattle of dry undergrowth brought Carl from his napping.

"Hey, George?"

"Over here," Dan answered.

"You going to work that brush?"

"Figure to," Ragan said, and then, deciding suddenly to gamble and perhaps rid themselves of the rider, added: "You keep looking on that side. Meet you on the flat."

"Sure," Carl said, apparently both pleased and relieved. "Be waiting for you at the shack."

The trees were abruptly all around them, tall, ghostly shapes in the pale light of the stars. Ragan drew to a halt, ears cocked into the darkness. Off to their right he could hear Carl's horse as it plodded wearily on down the trail; he could expect no more problems from that source, Dan realized, but such was scant relief. He now needed to be concerned with Gates and Lasater, somewhere off to their left.

"Are we going to stop here?" Ann asked hopefully.

She was dead tired. He was aware of that, but he was also conscious of the urgent need to get off the butte where they were being hunted, lose themselves somewhere in the valley below until time for Earl and the Mason City lawmen to arrive.

"Wish we could," he said. "Best we get out of here, clear of this part of the country. Too big a chance for us running into some of Chandler's outfit. Can rest a bit if you like. Oughtn't lose much time, however."

"I can go on," she said in a dogged tone.

He took her at her word and, touching the weary horse with spurs, headed deeper into the trees, picking out the shadowy aisles that appeared to be, in themselves, winding shadows of faintest silver.

They pressed on steadily, the horse gradually showing signs of his double load and the long day's use. Somewhere around midnight they reached the bottom, having had but one alarm—a stealthy noise off to one side followed by what sounded like the stamp of another weary horse. But nothing came of it, and Ragan, unwilling to spend any time investigating, accepted his assumption that it had likely been an animal of some sort—a deer probably, frightened from its bed. And thus they had continued on their way.

Keeping to the now thinning spur of trees that thrust out into the valley as well as the more prevalent brush, Ragan swung wide of the butte and pointed into the general direction of the Buckman ranch—or what remained of it.

He'd find a spot somewhere near where he could watch for the riders from Mason City, and then bed down for the balance of the night. Ann had to have rest, and he, too, was beginning to feel the drag of the hours, the hard riding, the dull ache in his leg.

Reaching the fringe of a small clearing, he halted, raised himself in the stirrups, and tried to locate himself, gauge the distance to Buckman's. The bluff was to his right, almost directly opposite now, and well to the west. Buckman's should lie due east, more or less. If he continued. . . .

"Ragan . . . don't move!" Jody Strickland's voice came from the dense brush no more than a stride away. "I've got my gun pointing right at your head."

XVIII

Dan Ragan sat perfectly still for a long breath, and then slowly his shoulders went down. He'd tried—and he'd failed. The boy had caught up with him despite all his efforts, and now there would be another killing. It was clear nothing had changed. Jody was still possessed with the same burning hate, the same unyielding desire to avenge his father—a man he did not really know.

"All right," he said quietly. "It's your way. Go easy with that iron. Got a girl on this horse with me."

"Know that. Been trailing along with you for two, three hours waiting for the chance to catch you in the open. Who is she?"

"A friend."

"Expect you're meaning the wife of a friend," Strickland said from the blackness in which he stood. "I knew when I seen all them cowpokes beating the brush up there that I'd find you, with somebody's woman, at the bottom of it."

"You're wrong, same as before," Ragan said patiently. "But there's no use telling you that."

"Which makes you right. I don't believe nothing you say . . . never have, never will. I know you, Ragan, know you good."

"Sure, Jody. Is it all right if we climb down off this horse?"

"It's all right . . . only don't try no tricks. Hate to drill you from here. I'm looking to standing out in the daylight so's you can see my bullet coming."

Dan shook his head, shifted to one side of the saddle. He felt Ann's arms release their grip around his waist. She was trembling.

"It's going to be all right," he said, swinging down. Reaching up, he caught her under the arms, lifted her easily from the horse. Turning then, he faced the shadows in which Strickland was hiding.

"This lady is Ann Buckman . . . Miss Buckman . . . Jody. Owns a ranch east of here."

Strickland laughed. "You sure she ain't somebody's wife?"

"I'm sure. And keep your voice down. I don't want that bunch you saw coming down on our backs."

Strickland said: "Neither do I. You're my meat, Ragan. Ain't nobody going to cheat me out of squaring things for my pa."

Dan, hands well away from his sides and in full view, laughed dryly. "You'll get your chance, Jody. I'm through running from you . . . something I was doing for your sake, not mine. I don't want to kill you."

Strickland laughed.

Ragan's temper lifted slightly. "You lose your manners along with your good sense? I introduced you to a lady. Be decent enough to step out here where she can see you."

The brush rustled, and a moment later Strickland, pistol in hand, moved into the weak light. He stared at the girl from round, sullen eyes.

"Pleased to meet you, ma'am," he mumbled.

"Well, I'm not pleased to meet you!" Ann snapped in an angry tone. "You're making a mistake hounding Dan Ragan like you are."

"I can see he's been talking to you."

"I know all about it . . . and you're wrong. You should have listened to that marshal. Your father was no good. He deserved killing. And you're going to get yourself killed, too, if you. . . ."

"Don't worry about me none, ma'am," Jody broke in. "I ain't no baby. I know what I'm doing."

"Maybe you're no baby, but you act like one! Dan's trying to do you a favor, be kind to you."

"I don't want none of his favors. All I'm wanting is to square things for my pa."

"Your father doesn't deserve your giving up your life. What that marshal told you about him was the truth."

"The marshal always had it in for Pa," Jody said stubbornly. "Was ag'in' him from the day he rode into that town. He would've stood up for Ragan no matter what happened."

"When was it you last saw your father . . . before he was shot?"

"Been maybe a year."

"Which all goes to prove what Dan and that marshal said!" Ann cried in exasperation. "You really didn't know a thing about him . . . what he was actually like!"

"Knew enough . . . and he was my pa. Might as well quit your yammering, ma'am, I aim. . . ."

"Can't you see I'm trying to save your life . . . keep you from getting killed?" Ann took an involuntary step toward the boy. "Dan doesn't want to hurt you. Can't you understand that?"

"Maybe he won't kill me. Maybe it'll be the other way around. Anyway, I aim to have my chance."

"You'll get it," Ragan said, tired of all the talk. "Give you my word on that since there seems to be no way of changing your mind."

Strickland was staring at him suspiciously. "Word? What're you giving me your word for?"

"Got a job to finish first. This lady's having big trouble over her ranch, and. . . ."

"Now, hold on here! I ain't figuring to. . . ."

"You're going to stand by and wait until I've done what I can for her," Ragan said in a low, firm voice. "You think you can keep me from it, then you'll have to put a bullet in my back."

There was a long minute of silence. Finally Jody said: "What've you got to do?"

"Get back to her ranch first. A rancher around here is trying to take over the whole valley. He wants her place so bad he's already killed her brother, burned all the buildings to the ground."

"Ain't nothing you can do about that."

"No, but we've sent for the law. He'll be riding in with some help around the middle of the morning. Got to see that she gets her chance to talk to him."

Again there was silence as Jody considered that. "Them 'punchers up there on top of the bluff, they working for this here rancher you're talking about?"

"All of them. Drove us off the place. We made a run for the butte, looking for a place to hide until dark. He had about a dozen of them beating the brush."

"Watched them. Was four of them coming, nosing over to where I'd camped. Seen them coming and lit out. Man never knows what's up when a bunch like that's running loose."

"I heard them talking about your campfire. They figured it was Indians. I reckon that was you in the brush we heard coming down the slope, too."

"Sure was. Had to get myself a close look, be sure it was you. Was too dark there on the butte. I. . . ."

"Stop it! Stop it!" Ann broke in suddenly in a wild, frenzied voice. "What's the matter with you two?"

Jody stared at her. "Matter?"

"You stand here, talking like friends passing the time of day, while all the time you're planning to shoot it out . . . kill each other. One of you will die. Maybe the both of you. What kind of men are you?"

Dan slid an arm around the girl. She was near hysterics and he comforted her by drawing her close, patting her gently on the shoulder. He glanced at Jody.

"Put that damned gun away . . . I gave you my word. Next

thing is . . . do you want to sit in this game, give the lady a hand, or do you want to stand around and wait until I'm through helping her?"

Strickland shook his head. "Can't see as it's any of my put-in. And far as stepping aside, waiting, I ain't sure I'm agreeing. . . ."

"You will anyway. Things are working out to where you'll have to sort of get in line."

"What's that mean?"

"I've got a gun slick name of Korello looking to settle with me, too. Knew him a time back. Now he's working for this rancher, Chandler, I was telling you about."

Jody wagged his head vigorously. "Now, see here, I ain't backing off for nobody. . . ."

"Then you'd best string along with us," Ragan said, and, turning to Ann, took her by the arm and helped her onto the horse. Bluntly ignoring Strickland, he went to the saddle, pointed his mount for the Buckman ranch. "About the only way you can protect your interests, it seems to me," he added with a grin.

XIX

It was still dark when they halted in a small grove of cottonwood trees a short distance above the Buckman place. Fires still glowed in the yard of the ruined ranch, and in the feeble starlight the skeletons of walls yet standing here and there were stark reminders of what once had been. Smoke hung low over the land, seemingly reluctant to lift, float away, and thus reveal the destruction. Even in the scatter of cottonwoods, there was the harsh smell of cremated leather mixed with the odors of charred wood, destroyed clothing, and all the other items that had gone up in the flames.

Dismounting, Ragan helped Ann from the horse, and, pointing to a nearby, grass-floored coulée, said: "Be a good spot for you to get some rest."

She nodded absently, moved to the tiny basin, and sat down. He watched her for a moment, noting her absolute weariness, feeling the hopelessness that gripped her, and conscious, too, of the cold that was causing her to shiver. He wished he had a coat or something to offer her, but he had nothing. And they could not risk a campfire.

"Won't be long until sunup," he said. "Be warm then."

At that point Jody Strickland stepped forward. He had removed his woolen brush jacket. Now he handed it to her.

"Maybe this'll help some."

Ann accepted it gravely, thanked him, and drew it on quickly. Ragan nodded to the boy, and moved off to the edge of the grove where, from the fringe of rabbit brush and other rank growth that ringed the oasis of trees, he had a good view of the Buckman place.

One fire, larger than the dozen or more others spotting the area, was near the north edge of the yard. As his glance halted upon it, he saw a figure rise from the shadows close by, pick up several lengths of wood, and toss them into the dwindling flames.

Dan grinned wryly. He hadn't figured on Chandler's maintaining a watch over the place. He had come close to riding in, having a close look, when they came in from the bluff, but some inner caution had warned him against it.

He remembered hearing Chandler's men speak of a meeting—a rendezvous—to be held that morning at the Buckman ranch. The exact time had not been mentioned. It would work out fine for Ann, if the sheriff and his men from Mason City happened to be around when the congregating took place. The lawman would be in a position to hear all he needed to arrest the cattleman.

The restless man at the fire settled down. As a brighter glow spread around him, he leaned back against a log, began to roll a cigarette. Completed, he lit it with a brand from the fire, once again relaxed. The broader flare of light from the replenished flames revealed two more blanketed forms, and the thought came to Dan that Ross Chandler had left the place well guarded, and set him to wondering why.

It could only be that the rancher intended to be certain no Buckman, or anyone connected with them, was left alive to tell the story of what had transpired. Chandler's plan was simply to wipe out the Buckmans and all evidence of their being, or ever having been, in Lagrima Valley. And it was possible for him, the only other occupant of the surrounding 200 square miles or more. There would be no one to wonder about the Buckmans, and ask questions.

Swearing softly, he wheeled about, came fully into Jody Strickland, only a step or two behind him in the brush.

"Scared I'll pull out on you?" he demanded, angry.

Jody shrugged. "Ain't taking no chances."

"Worrying for nothing, boy. I'll keep my word. But you stay clear of me until I've settled with Korello and got things lined up with the sheriff. Understand?"

Strickland nodded, drew to one side for Ragan to pass. "You needing help?"

Dan said—"Up to you."—and returned to the coulée.

Ann was sleeping, restless and uncomfortable, but sleeping nevertheless. He realized then his own weariness and, moving to the base of a large tree, sat down, back to the thick trunk. Through half-shut eyes he saw Jody enter the basin, vaguely heard the barking of a coyote far, far in the distance, it seemed.

He came awake with a start. It was still night but a pale glow was showing in the sky behind him. It would not be long until sunrise. He glanced at the girl. She had not stirred, a testimonial to her exhaustion.

Directly opposite Jody Strickland, with hunched shoulders to a cottonwood, watched him with unrelenting eyes. The boy was not putting much faith in the promise that had been made, Dan thought, and wondered if he had slept at all but had just sat there keeping his stubborn vigilance during the minutes—or was it hours?—that he had garnered a little rest.

Rising quietly so as not to disturb Ann, Ragan strode by Jody and made his way again to the brush at the edge of the grove. It was light enough now to see that not three but four men had remained in the Buckman yard during the night.

Two of the riders were up, moving about. One was building a fire, the other digging into his saddlebags, apparently in quest of food. He could use a little food himself, Dan realized, and undoubtedly Ann was in need, too, although she had made no complaint.

Without turning, he said: "You got any grub in your gear?"

There was a moment before Jody, not expecting the question, replied: "Some. Hard tack, jerky. Ain't carrying much."

"Dig it out. The lady'll be hungry."

Strickland started to turn away, hesitated. Ragan gave him an impatient frown. "For hell's sake, go on. I don't aim to go walking out there and tackle that bunch cold. The ones I want aren't there, anyway."

Strickland walked away, headed back for the coulée. Dan swung his attention back to Chandler's men. The others were up now, hunched around the fire, warding off the chill as they had their first smokes and waited for the first cheering rays of sun. There was no talking, as is usual at such hour, only a grumpy silence.

After a few minutes Ragan returned to the clearing, found Jody had brought out his store of trail food, was laying it out for Ann. She looked up at his approach, smiled.

"We have hard biscuits and dried meat for breakfast, thanks to Jody. He has water, too." She paused, added wistfully: "I don't suppose we dare build a fire."

"It'd be a mistake," he said, and, taking one of the biscuits between his palms, crushed it into several pieces. Handing it back to the girl, he said: "Little easier to eat this way. Washes down better."

No more was said after that, and they finished the meal, if such it could be termed, in a short time. Rising, anxious to return to the brush where he could see what was developing in the yard, Dan nodded to Jody.

"Obliged to you. Was in need of that."

Strickland grinned, said: "Sure. Condemned man's always treated to a last meal before dying."

Ragan's eyes dropped to the girl. He saw her lips tighten and a shudder pass through her, and then she began to gather up the remainder of the food.

"Not thanking you for that," he said, and moved on toward the brush.

He expected to hear Jody add more comment along a similar vein and was surprised to hear him say instead: "I'm sorry, ma'am. Didn't mean for that to upset you none."

"It's all right," Ann replied quietly. "I wish you and Dan could settle your differences . . . be friends."

"Not much chance of us ever being friends. Sure aim to do some settling with him."

"You're wrong about him, Jody . . . about what happened. You don't really know. . . ."

Ragan continued on out of hearing. Ann was wasting her breath. Jody had made up his mind, then closed and locked it as effectively as if he'd dropped a bar across a door. Nothing Ann could say would ever make any difference.

The sun was out, its warm light now stealing swiftly and

silently over the land, washing away the shadows, stirring all things into motion.

The four men at the fire were boiling up a can of coffee, and the odor of it, drifting to Dan Ragan, set him to hungering for a cup. That desire was quickly forgotten in the next moment when, coming in from the west, he saw two riders break out of the brush, point for the camp. It was Korello and his partner, Toby. Evidently they had spent the night guarding the foot of the trail.

Sour-faced and in ill humor, the gunman and his partner entered the circle, silently helped themselves to the coffee. A man squatting on his heels across the fire looked up as Korello drained his cup.

Korello shook his head briefly, reached for the can of coffee again. "They didn't come down that wash. Don't think they were ever up there in the first place. When's Chandler coming?"

"Didn't say. Prob'ly be a couple hours yet. Said we was to wait here."

"Pretty soft, him sleeping home in a warm bed, us laying out here, freezing our tails. . . ."

"My sentiments, too, only I ain't about to do no yelping. You figure to?"

"Just could be I will," Korello said and paused, his eyes halting on riders coming in from the north. In the lead were George and Carl, riding double. A short distance behind them were the two others who had been on the plateau, Gates and Lasater.

One of the men at the fire observed unnecessarily: "George's gone and lost his horse, seems."

"Looks like they didn't have no luck, either," another remarked. "Ross sure ain't going to like what he's going to get told this morning."

Ragan drew back into the brush. All of Chandler's men who had been on the butte were accounted for and now awaited the rancher's arrival. And there was still no sign of Sheriff McGaffey and the men he was supposed to bring from Mason City. Unless they showed up soon—before Ross Chandler put in his appearance.

His thoughts broke off as more riders loomed up to the north beyond a low ridge and bore in at a steady clip. A heaviness settled over him as he recognized the man in the center. It was Ross Chandler. Shrugging, Dan turned, started back for the coulée. He guessed he could forget his hope of having McGaffey on hand, being an actual witness to Chandler's ruthless activities. He'd have to come up with another idea.

XX

He reached the coulée, moved on by, and made his way to the south edge of the grove. So deep was he in thought he did not notice until he had stopped that both Ann Buckman and Strickland had followed.

"What is it?" she asked at once, turned anxious by the tautness of his features.

"Chandler's coming, along with the rest of his outfit. Doubt if they'll hang around long. Was hoping that sheriff'd be here so's we could force Chandler to tip his hand, prove all the things you'll be telling about him."

Grim, he stared out across the low hills running indefinitely into the south. The ruts that were the road leading to Mason City were a tan scar on the darker brown of the undisturbed soil. The horizon was empty.

"Reckon we'll have to do without him."

She did not understand. "How can we? The sheriff should be here to listen, make an arrest, shouldn't he?"

Ragan's shoulders stirred. "One of those times when you have to take matters into your own hands. Happens kind of regular in this country."

Jody Strickland's jaw was set. "What're you going to do?"

"If that lawman isn't here by the time Chandler and his bunch are ready to pull out, then the only thing I can do is show myself, force them into staying put until. . . ."

"You mean you'll be getting out there, maybe putting on a shoot-out with this Korello?"

"Whatever it takes," Ragan said.

Strickland wagged his head. "No deal. I won't. . . ."

Ann, looking anxiously to the south, broke in: "The sheriff should be here by now, don't you think?"

"No way of knowing for sure. If your brother got there when I figured he would . . . early last night . . . and if McGaffey and his men mounted up and started back inside an hour or so, then they ought to be showing up."

"A lot of ifs," Jody commented.

"Earl would have insisted they start right away," Ann said, ignoring the remark. "He would tell them how bad everything was here, and he'd not let them rest until they got under way. I know how he is."

"Could be that sheriff wasn't even in town," Strickland said. "You think of that?"

Ragan had, but he didn't feel it was necessary to mention it to the girl. A lawman's county under territorial government was usually far-flung, and a conscientious sheriff was out of his office a considerable amount of the time.

"Be a deputy on duty," he said. "He'd act for the sheriff." Drawing his pistol, he thumbed aside the loading gate, spun the cylinder, and checked the cartridges. Taking a shell from his belt, he filled the ordinarily empty sixth chamber. As a matter of common sense and personal safety, he kept the pistol's hammer resting on the blank space, but with everything pointing to a confrontation with Chandler and his men—his one gun against a dozen or more—he wanted as much going for him as possible.

Thrusting the weapon back into its holster, lifting it, and allowing it to fall several times as he tested its smoothness in coming from the leather, he looked down at Ann.

"I want you to stay here, wait for McGaffey. It's time I was getting out there, doing what I can toward keeping them busy until he shows up."

A frown pulled at the girl's features as concern flooded her eyes suddenly. "No, Dan . . . I don't want you to. The ranch doesn't mean that much to me. Please, let it go. Let's just leave. . . ."

"Somebody coming now," Strickland announced. "Could be your lawman."

Ragan whirled, threw his glance to the road. A half dozen riders were topping out one of the ridges. Even at the great distance he could recognize the tall, blaze-faced bay he had lent Earl Buckman to make the ride. They were coming—but agonizingly slowly.

"Got to get them over here," he said, swinging back to Ann. "Want you to take the horse, ride out and meet them. Keep close to the edge of those foothills on the left and you won't be seen. . . ."

The girl nodded, turned, ran toward the horse they had earlier taken from Chandler's man. Dan was close beside her, boosted her onto the saddle.

"Tell McGaffey to ease in quiet, stay in the brush out of sight but close enough to hear what's said. He'll know when to show himself."

Ann's eyes were filled with concern, her face stiff with worry as she moved her head again in understanding. Wheeling the horse about, she swung in beside Ragan. Leaning over, she kissed him on the lips.

"Be careful, Dan," she murmured softly, and headed her mount off into the brush.

Immediately Ragan pivoted and started for the yard. Strickland caught at his arm as if to stay him. He shook the younger man off, hurried on. When he reached the fringe of brush, relief poured through him. Chandler and his men were still there.

"One hell of a note!" the rancher was saying in a scarcely controlled, raging voice. "A woman and a saddle tramp getting away from the lot of you! And on foot! What the devil were you all doing, picking daisies?"

"Got dark," Korello said bluntly. "Ain't none of us owls, we couldn't see nothing. Ain't so sure they ever went up on that butte, anyway."

"Then where'd they go?" Chandler demanded. "Sure didn't just fade into thin air. God dammit, I want them found and put out of the way. Worked too long getting this valley shaped up to where it's all mine to let them mess up my plans!"

"Maybe you'd better be doing some looking yourself," Korello said dryly. "You figure it's easy . . . try your hand."

Several of the riders glanced at the gunman, shifted nervously at his hard words. Ross Chandler stared at Korello, lips pulled down into a tight, gray line while anger held him to a rigid stance.

"Just what I aim to do," he said in slow, well-spaced words. "Always knew when a man wanted something important done, he'd best do it himself . . . not depend on the hired help. And while I'm thinking of it, when we're done, you and me've got some talking to do. Final talking."

"Any time," Korello replied indifferently.

Chandler whirled, started for his horse. "All right, mount up! Want every brush clump in this valley kicked over. . . ."

"No need!" Ragan called in a loud voice, and strode casually into the open. "I'm right here."

The rancher halted, spun, a curse exploding from his lips. Several of the riders drew up sharply, hands reaching for their weapons, and then falling away as they saw the six-gun already in Dan's hand. Only Jim Korello seemed undisturbed by Ragan's appearance.

"You . . . the god-damn' drifter!" Chandler yelled, recovering. He swept his men with a withering glance. "He was here all the time . . . right under your noses . . . and you couldn't spot him! What the hell kind of jaybirds I got working for me . . . ?" The rancher broke off with a helpless shake of his head. Then, squaring himself around, he faced Ragan. "You're a damn' fool. Reckon you know that, don't you? I give the word to cut you down, and you're dead. You ain't holding off a dozen guns alone. . . ."

"He ain't alone." Jody Strickland's voice came from the thick brush to Dan's right. "Way I got it figured, standing in here, I'm making the odds about even."

Chandler and his men again showed surprise. The rancher swallowed hard, squinted at the clump of undergrowth.

"Who the hell are you, cutting yourself in this way?"

"No friend of Ragan's, if that's what you're getting at. Only aim to see he comes out of this with a whole skin."

Chandler frowned. "That don't make no sense."

"Don't need to. Just keep remembering I'm here covering you."

Chandler wagged his head, muttered: "Still don't make sense. Just what you aim . . . ?"

"Forget him," Dan cut in. "It's me you've got to deal with."

"For a fact," the rancher said, bringing his attention back to Ragan. "Where's the Buckman woman? She with you?"

"Got her waiting back in the trees."

"Trot her out here. Want to get this thing all wound up today."

"How? By putting a bullet in her like you did her brother?"

"If need be," Chandler said coolly. "Made him an offer for

the place. He was too stump-headed to listen. Didn't leave me no choice."

"So whoever won't go along with what you want gets plowed under."

"Good way to put it. Only going to be one ranch in this valley when I'm finished, and that's mine."

"That's why you killed Pogue Buckman and burned down his place. It's the only one that didn't belong to you."

Chandler nodded. "Like I said, I was willing to make a deal with the Buckmans. When I couldn't get nowheres, I done what I had to."

"Still two of them left . . . the sister and the younger brother. What about them?"

The rancher glanced around at the charred remains of the ranch buildings. "Ain't much here for them to hang onto now. Reckon they'll listen."

"What if they won't?"

Chandler shrugged. "Bullet out of a gun don't care what it hits . . . man, woman . . . or a kid."

"Not when you're behind it," Ragan said slowly. "And that's just what you've got waiting for them, same as you've got for me . . . a bullet. After what you've done, you can't risk letting any of us stay alive."

The rancher glanced toward his men, shook his head. "Ain't that way a-tall. I make a deal, give my word to anybody. Korello . . . Gates . . . now!"

Dan saw the gunman lurch forward, saw the glint of sunlight on his pistol as it came up. Beyond him the man called Gates was a blur of motion, also. Throwing himself to one side, he triggered his weapon twice, hearing the rap of other shots as he did.

Korello staggered to one side, went to his knees, an angry frown on his face. Behind him Gates also was down, smoke trickling from the gun lying beside him. A third man was clutching his arm as blood slowly stained the sleeve of his shirt. All the others remained frozen. He owed Jody Strickland for some help. He'd fired only twice—Korello and Gates. Jody had accounted for the third man.

Grim, taut as steel wire, he stared at Chandler. "You got anybody else you'd like to have try?"

The rancher and his riders were standing in silence, looking at something beyond him. Ragan turned his head cautiously. Half a dozen men had drawn up at the edge of the yard. Sunlight glinted off the stars pinned to their vests.

Off to the left young Earl Buckman was beside his sister. Dan could see the relief on her face, either for the arrival of the lawmen, or because he had come safely through the encounter with Chandler's gun hawks. He wasn't sure which, and it didn't matter. He was just glad it was over.

"You hear all you need to, Sheriff?" he called.

The hard-faced man, wearing crossed belts with twin ivory-handled Colts riding high in their holsters, touched his horse with his heels, circled the charcoal ruin of the Buckman house, and, closely followed by his deputies, drew to a halt alongside Ragan.

"Reckon I have," the lawman said. "Howsomever, I didn't aim to let things go as far as they did. I was going to step in earlier when Chandler there'd said enough to. . . ."

The rancher moved forward, face contorted with anger. "Now, see here, Sheriff, you know me. I'm. . . ."

"Sure, I know you," McGaffey interrupted. "You're the man who's going to spend a few years in the pen at Santa Fé . . . or may even hang. That answer your question?"

Ross Chandler had halted, was staring at the lawman as if unable to believe his own ears. He glanced at the men ranged around him, apparently wondering if he dared make a fight of it. He evidently decided it would be a losing battle. "All right," he muttered, and looked down.

McGaffey made a motion to his deputies. "Pull their irons and shackle them. We'll take 'em all back to Mason City and sort them out there. All over with here."

"Not yet," Jody Strickland said, stepping into the open. "Got a score of my own to settle with Ragan. Want you to see it's all done fair and square."

XXI

The lawman stared, watched Jody walk into the center of the cleared ground. At once Ann Buckman, closely followed by Earl, hurried to Ragan's side.

"You've got to stop them!" she cried, facing the sheriff. "They're going to kill each other . . . and it's all a mistake!"

McGaffey climbed down from his horse, placed his glance on Dan. There was a puzzled look in his eyes.

"Mind telling me what's going on? Wasn't that young fellow there siding you?"

Ragan permitted himself a dry smile. "Sided me because he wanted to keep me alive. Now he wants a shoot-out."

The lawman scrubbed at his jaw, slowly wagged his head. "Loco kind of a thing. Why's he gunning for you?"

"Little trouble I had with his pa."

"Kill him?"

Ragan nodded.

Ann took a step nearer the sheriff. "Jody's got the wrong idea. He thinks Dan shot his father for the wrong reasons. He thinks his father was a good man . . . but he wasn't. You can ask the marshal. . . ."

The words were pouring from the girl, coming in a wild rush, stumbling upon each other as she endeavored to make McGaffey understand. Dan touched her arm, drew her back.

"I've been ducking this thing since it got started. I don't want a showdown with him. He's just a boy and I don't have anything against him. But I'm tired of running, dodging. I figure I might as well settle it here."

"No!" Ann cried. "You won't be honest with yourself! You'll hold back because you feel sorry for him! You'll get yourself killed!"

"No need of him doing that," Jody said. "I reckon I can hold up my end of it."

"Then you're pretty good," McGaffey said coolly. "You look sort of familiar. I know you from somewhere? You got a name?"

"Strickland."

The lawman's head came up sharply. "Strickland," he repeated. "Strickland . . . ? You know a man, a gambler name of Colby Strickland? Some called him Acey-Deucy Strickland."

"He was my pa," Jody replied. "Was he a friend of yours, too?"

"Friend!" McGaffey spat out the word. "He got out of my town about three years ago five minutes ahead of a lynching party! Folks around there and a few other places on west of Mason City would still like to get their paws on him."

"You sure we're talking about the same man?" Jody's voice was strained, almost as if he dreaded to hear the answer.

"Expect so. He was a tall fellow, good looker. Had a way with the women. Always wore a moustache trimmed short."

The boy's eyes were on the ground. "That's him, all right. What kind of trouble was he in?"

"Always something, usually slickering somebody in a card game. What nigh got him lynched was that he put the daughter of one of the townsfolk into a family way, then wouldn't marry her. Girl hung herself." McGaffey paused, his weathered face drawn into a dark frown. "Is that what this is all about? You want to go up against this man here because he shot Colby

Strickland? Hell, he ought to get a vote of thanks for doing it . . . and I expect he had good reason. Son or not, boy, you're a plain fool looking to avenge a man like Strickland. He's not worth it."

Jody did not raise his head. In the hush that dropped over the yard only the restless shifting of the horses could be heard.

"I'm sorry about it, Jody," Ragan said, breaking the silence. "That's the kind he was. Tried to tell you that, same as the marshal. Expect you were too worked up to listen. But if you still figure you have to have it out, then I'm ready. I'm not running any more."

Jody Strickland shook his head, turned away. "Forget it," he murmured, and started toward his horse.

A cry of relief burst from Ann Buckman's lips. She wheeled, threw herself into Dan Ragan's arms.

"Oh . . . I'm so glad . . . so relieved!"

Ragan, never fully letting down his caution, watched Jody swing onto the saddle and, eyes downcast, disillusionment and defeat holding him in a tight grasp, ride from the yard. Only then did the tautness begin to slip from Dan's frame.

"So am I," he answered, and shifted his attention to the lawman and his deputies busily engaged in the process of getting Chandler and his riders ready for the trip back to Mason City. His glance wandered on, swept the blackened embers, the destruction that was the ranch.

"We've got us a big mess here. Take a powerful lot of work to fix things up, get the place going again."

Smiling, eyes filled with hope, Ann looked at him. "Us?"

"All three of us," he said.

★ ★ ★ ★ ★

Fire Valley

★ ★ ★ ★ ★

I

When the stagecoach reached the edge of town and whirled into the dusty main street, Dave Ruskin heaved a sigh. It had been a long, hot ride from Laramie, and he'd been the lone passenger since Denver.

Now he pulled himself forward on the seat, glanced through the window at the rows of false-fronted, weather-beaten buildings lining the way. Up on the box the driver shouted a greeting to several men standing on the plank sidewalk, and then the brakes slammed against the iron tires of the wheels, going on and off, setting up a harsh grating as they slowed the vehicle.

Apache Wells. It looked to be a pretty good town—little different from the scores of others he'd passed through or tarried in during his wanderings across the frontier. It boasted a bank, a number of saloons, a hotel, café, the usual stores dominant among which was one bearing the sign: *Yates Merchandise Emporium.* Residences were scattered along the fringe of the larger structures, and off to one side in lonely dignity stood a small, steepled church, its elevated cross etched against the clean sky.

There appeared to be quite a few persons about, a celebration of some sort, he thought, or perhaps it was Saturday—the end of the week when ranchers brought their families in for shopping. He tried to remember—was it Saturday? He'd lost track of time, but he guessed it didn't really matter. The surprising thing was that he was there at all.

Two weeks ago he'd been riding fence for Tom Jefferies up

Wyoming way, the latest of many jobs he'd held during the past ten years of drifting. And then the letter from J. Phillips, Esq., a lawyer, had caught up with him and everything changed. A long-forgotten uncle, Saul Gans, had died, willed to him his property. It was unbelievable! He'd read the letter over a dozen times before it finally sank in—he had a spread of his own. No more working for forty a month and found, no more pointless wandering, no more sleeping in flea-bit hotels, drafty bunkhouses, or rolled up in a blanket on some wind-swept flat. From then on it would be a decent place to live, regular meals, cattle—a place where he could put down roots once and for all time.

It was like a dream. He couldn't recall ever having seen Saul Gans, a brother of his mother's, but he did remember the faded, old daguerreotype that stood on a chest of drawers in his parents' bedroom. It pictured a squat, thick-necked man with heavy features and a large, sweeping moustache. Recalling scraps of information and overheard bits of conversation from his childhood, he gathered that Uncle Saul wasn't much good, a family black sheep, and one his mother would have as soon forgotten.

His pa, however, had evidently liked Saul, had gone so far as to lend him a little of the hard-earned cash grubbed from the soil of their Missouri farm—a loan to help Gans get started out west somewhere. It was money down a rat hole, he'd heard his mother declare more than once during their periodic and usually heated references to it.

Apparently it was. Time passed. The war broke out, raged, and ended, and no word came from Saul Gans. He was probably dead, scalped by Indians likely, they both decided. And when both died years later, Dave, a mature sixteen at the time, had accepted the assumption and gone on his way.

Now, a decade later, Saul Gans was again in his mind—and

very much a real person. All property belonging to the said Saul Gans has been willed to you, so the letter from J. Phillips, Esq., had stated, along with the suggestion that he proceed at once to Apache Wells, Territory of New Mexico, present the letter and other enclosed papers to the authorities in that settlement, and claim his inheritance.

Stunned by such good fortune from a source he'd long forgotten, Dave had quit his Wyoming job, sold his horse and gear, and bought a ticket south after dispatching a postal card to the foreman of the ranch requesting that he be met at the stage depot on a specified day.

All during the tedious miles down from Laramie he tried not to think too much about the ranch—his ranch. It could prove to be nothing, a hard-rock, starved-out patch hardly worth getting, but it would be something—and it was his. That was the important thing; good, bad, or worthless, it was his. And it could be made to pay if handled right. His pa had drilled that into him over and over. As long as a man was willing to work, he'd come out all right.

The coach jolted to a stop in front of the small building housing the office of the Southwestern Stage Lines. The driver began to climb down from his perch, yelling to a man who came from around the side of the structure. Ruskin reached for the door handle, turned it, and stepped out into the hot sunshine.

"Apache Wells, mister." The driver grinned, mopping at the sweat on his face. "What you been looking for."

Dave, a tall, lean man with dark eyes and hair, drew himself up to ease his tired muscles, nodded, and glanced about. People along the walk had paused to stare, eye him critically. A short, graying man wearing black satin sleeve guards and an eyeshade was coming from the interior of the building carrying a U.S. Mail sack. Hostlers were changing the team. All seemed to be taking more than ordinary interest in the arrival of a stranger.

Ruskin shrugged off the thought, walked to the rear of the coach, and pulled his blanket roll from the boot. In it, except for the clothes he wore and the pistol belted around his waist, was everything he owned—that plus $87 currency he had in his shirt pocket.

" 'Luck," the driver said, squinting at him as he turned to enter the office. "Hotel's right down the street."

He wouldn't need a room, not this time. Stepping up onto the walk, he probed the street. Directly opposite, in the shade of a broadly spreading cottonwood, an old cowhand was slumped on the seat of a buckboard. Leathery face turned to Dave, he raised a hand.

"You Ruskin?"

Dave bobbed his head. "You from the Gans place?"

"Reckon I am," the oldster said. Settling back and taking up the reins, he swung the buckboard around and halted in front of Dave. Shifting the worn leathers to his left hand, he extended his right.

"Folks call me Link . . . Link Henry. Veetch sent me down to fetch you."

Ruskin tossed his blanket roll into the bed of the light wagon, closed his fingers about those of Henry.

"Veetch?" he said, climbing onto the seat.

"Your ramrod . . . Jess Veetch. Reckoned he couldn't come, sent me."

"All the same to me, long as I don't have to walk," Dave said. "Sounds like things at the ranch are right busy."

Link Henry spat, stared off down the street. "Ain't that."

Ruskin frowned, looked more closely at the older man. "Trouble?"

Henry turned, faced Dave. "Ain't one for talking out about such things, but you're asking, so I'm telling. Jess and some of his boys've got themselves a card game going. Just didn't want to break it up."

Anger spurted through Dave Ruskin. You'd think a foreman could find time to welcome the new boss, especially when he wasn't busy—and then he brushed his impatience aside. He guessed there really wasn't anything wrong with the foreman's delegating the chore to someone else. A man could get to playing poker, be having a fine run of luck. Still—the middle of the afternoon—a card game—nobody working.

"I take it things are a mite quiet."

Henry wagged his head. "Worse'n that. Ain't been nothing doing since Saul died . . . nothing." The old man paused, squinted into the glaring sunlight. "Howsomever, looks mighty like things are going to start happening right now. Here comes a whole passel of folks to see you, and it ain't pleasure they got in mind."

II

Ruskin lifted his glance. The group of men he'd noticed earlier, now headed by a tall, lanky individual wearing a star on his shield shirt, was moving up to the buckboard. Other onlookers along the walk had stopped to watch, some falling in behind the party.

"Now, what the hell you reckon they're wanting?" Link Henry wondered.

Dave studied the approaching men narrowly. "Know them?"

Henry nodded. "Lawman's Harvey Drace. Big redhead walking next to him is Floyd Trigg. Owns the Circle Eight outfit, east of here. One by him's another rancher, name of Rufe Hyatt. The old man, one with the white eyebrows and moustache, is Amos Pool. His Tumbling A spread is north of yours. That's Darrow . . . Eric Darrow . . . siding him. His is the E-Bar-D, up the other side of Trigg's. Rest of them's just local people, ogling and listening."

Ruskin eased back on the buckboard's hard seat. Whatever it was all about—it wasn't good. The ranchers and the town marshal appeared grim, even angry.

The group pulled to a halt, thinned out to form a half circle with Drace slightly forward. Beyond the cluster of ranchers and townspeople a girl in a white shirtwaist and corduroy skirt halted her buggy to watch, her soft-edged face sober and disturbed beneath its crown of dark hair.

"You Ruskin?" Harvey Drace's voice was hard, the question blunt.

Dave said: "That's me."

"You aiming to take over the Gans place?"

The lawman's attitude rubbed at Ruskin's nerves. "Any reason why I shouldn't?"

"Plenty!" the man pointed out as Rufe Hyatt spoke up angrily. "We've had all the. . . ."

The marshal lifted his arm hurriedly, pressed the rancher back. "Never mind, Rufe. I'll handle this."

"Somebody sure as hell had better!" Hyatt snapped. "I'm getting god damn' tired of losing stock."

Drace frowned at the cattleman. "Now, you don't know for sure Saul had anything to do with it."

"Maybe I don't . . . leastwise right at the moment. But I've got some proof . . . and soon as I'm certain. . . ."

"You come straight to me," the lawman broke in, and swung his attention back to Dave. "Reckon the best thing is to come to the point," he said after a moment. "Folks around here were hoping you'd not be moving in. Ain't nobody feels kindly toward the Gans outfit."

"Can't see as that has anything to do with me, but why?"

"Well, there's been some rustling going on . . . not a whole lot, just little bunches now and then. . . ."

"Been more than little bunches far as I'm concerned!" Floyd Trigg said, slamming his half-finished cigar to the ground. "I've lost aplenty."

"Same here," Darrow said. "Fifty head at least, so far this year."

A coolness came over Dave. "You accusing my uncle?"

"No . . . not exactly," Drace responded.

"Then maybe you'd better keep that kind of talk to yourself, Marshal, especially since he's not here to stand up for himself."

Drace shook his head. "Don't mean to speak bad of the dead, only saying what folks think. It's been going on for quite a spell, and it all points to Saul Gans and that bunch of hardcases and ex-convicts that work for him."

Ruskin glanced at Link Henry. The old cowpuncher's eyes were bright, his jaw set. He caught Dave's look, moved his head slightly.

Ruskin shrugged. "I'll ask it again, Marshal . . . have you got any proof?"

"Only what they. . . ."

"I don't give a damn what people say!" Dave snapped. "It's what they know that counts with me. Seems all you've got is hunches and rumors."

"You going to keep the same crew . . . Veetch and the whole bunch?" Hyatt demanded.

"Far as I know. Haven't met any of them yet, except Henry, here."

"Link's maybe all right. It's them others. . . ."

"Long as they're doing the job, they'll stay," Dave said, and then, suddenly aroused, added: "If you think I'm firing any man just because you don't like him, think again. I'll run my own outfit to suit myself."

Link Henry grunted a soft approval.

Harvey Drace pushed his hat to the back of his head. "Guess that's plain enough." He hesitated, covered the men around him with a quick glance. "Was told to make you an offer for your place, if you wasn't of a mind to listen to reason. Men here all got together and are willing to chip in, buy you out. They'll fork over five thousand in cash money if you'll sell them your ranch, and keep going."

"You keep the stock, sell it . . . do whatever you like," Hyatt added hurriedly. "Be a good deal for you, give you a nice piece of change without you ever turning a hand."

Dave stared beyond the waiting men to the girl in the buggy. She was watching him intently, almost eagerly. One of the ranchers' daughters, he guessed, and absently wondered which.

"What about it?" Drace pressed.

"Nope, guess not," Ruskin drawled. "Always wanted a place of my own. This is it."

"And you aim to keep right on, just the way Saul Gans was doing?"

"I figure to raise cattle," Dave replied quietly. "I'd like to do it among friends, but if that's not how you want it, then it'll have to be the other way."

"Meaning trouble," Harvey Drace murmured.

"Somebody else will start it. I won't."

"There'll be trouble, all right," Hyatt said in a resigned voice. Suddenly he took a long step forward. "I'm warning you, Ruskin!" he added, shaking his finger in Dave's face. "I miss one more steer, I'll get my crew together and pay you a call . . . one that sure'n hell won't be the sociable kind."

Drace reached out, laid a restraining hand on the rancher's shoulder. "Hold up a minute now, Rufe. Won't be none of that."

"The hell there won't!" Hyatt shouted, knocking the lawman's hand away. "Maybe you can't do nothing about what's been going on, but I sure can! I'm serving notice on you,

Ruskin . . . either you sell out to us or get rid of that bunch of owlhoots hanging around your place, or. . . ."

Rufe Hyatt paused. Dave leaned forward, his features taut. "Or . . . what?"

"Or me and some of the others'll take the law into our own hands and straighten things up. You got a choice."

Dave smiled thinly. "Maybe a choice, but I don't like people telling me what I have to do. Never was much of a hand at swallowing ultimatums . . . so I'll tell you this, Hyatt. You come riding into my place looking for trouble, I guarantee you'll find it."

Floyd Trigg swore, removed his hat, and ran a hand through his red hair. "Maybe we're going at this all wrong. We don't know Ruskin, and I figure we ought to give him a chance. Now, I been hurt bad as the rest of you, maybe more so, but I'm letting him alone, giving him time to straighten. . . ."

"Only way he can straighten things out is to get rid of that bunch Saul's had working for him, then burn the place down and start over from scratch. Been nothing but a pest hole from the beginning."

Eric Darrow shook his head. "You're a mite worked up, Rufe . . . and Floyd's right, partly."

"What's that mean?"

"Just this. Ruskin's new here, just moving in. Chances are he don't know nothing about anything, but I expect he's getting the idea now after all this yammering, so maybe he'll reconsider our offer . . . especially if we'll hike it a bit."

"What do you say, Ruskin?" Harvey Drace asked. "Want to change your mind?"

"No, thanks. I'll stay."

Darrow sighed gustily. Trigg shook his head. Amos Pool, his ruddy face shining with sweat, brushed nervously at his moustache.

"What about Saul's crew? You get rid of them and we'll do what we can to get you some good help."

"Even lend you a hand getting the place back in shape," Darrow added hopefully.

"Not interested," Ruskin said flatly, the aroused stubbornness within him refusing to yield even a trifle. If he had been approached differently, likely he would have seen reason with no difficulty, but to have it thrust at him, jammed down his throat, was something he could not abide.

"You're making a mistake . . . a big one," Harvey Drace murmured. "Take my advice. . . ."

"Mistake was on your side, with you and the rest," Dave cut in coldly.

The lawman nodded wearily. "I can see that now. But you can't blame them much. The way things've been going around here . . . rustlings, hold-ups, and such . . . everybody's about ready to jump sideways."

"They'll get no trouble from me," Dave said. "Just leave me be, let me run my ranch. It's all I'm asking."

"Nothing wrong with that. Long as you keep a tight rein on that wild bunch, nobody'll fault you. But the first time I catch. . . ."

"The first time," Ruskin interrupted, spacing his words clearly, "you've got something to back up your hunches, come, tell me. Being my men, I'll take the responsibility for them."

Drace cocked his head to one side. "All right, son, but before you go making a statement like that, you'd better trot out and meet them."

"Just what I figure to do," Dave said stiffly, and, turning to Link Henry, added: "Let's go."

III

The buckboard rolled past the silent group in the street, drew abreast the girl in the buggy, and swung onto the road west, its iron tires grating as they sliced into the loose sand. When they reached the last of the houses and began to bear into the low hill country, Dave Ruskin turned to Link.

"Seems I've got some real friendly folks for neighbors."

The old cowpuncher shrugged. "Reckon they got a call to be feeling that way."

Dave's jaw sagged. "You mean what they said was the truth?"

"Nope, ain't saying that. Leastwise, far as I know, it ain't. But they've been having plenty of trouble, and they just naturally look toward us. You know your uncle was a convict once?"

Surprise again rippled through Ruskin. He shook his head. "Hardly knew him at all. We . . . my folks and me . . . thought he was dead. Hadn't heard from him since before the war."

"Saul spent five years in the pen. Killed a man. Was self-defense, but the judge put him away just the same."

"Then there's something to this ex-convict thing . . . hiring them on as ranch hands, I mean?"

"Some. Old Saul sort of had a soft spot for a man who'd served time. Believed in giving him a chance to start over."

"Nothing wrong with that as long as they stay straight, keep their nose clean. This Jess Veetch . . . he one of them?"

"Nope."

The restraint in Link Henry's manner seemed to indicate everyone would be better off if the foreman was a convict and still behind bars, but he did not go into it.

Dave didn't press him. He stared out across the gently rising and falling hills, the slopes of which were blanketed and ablaze with the orange-flowered mallow plants from which Fire Valley took its name, and thought of what had been said by the ranchers and Harvey Drace.

"What about this rustling . . . their hinting that maybe Saul had something to do with it?"

"Nothing to it. He might've been hard as a hickory stump, but he was honest. And he watched things close. Had to, else he'd never built his place up from nothing more'n a lean-to in the middle of twenty thousand acres. He was no party to cattle rustling . . . I'd swear to that."

"What makes you so sure?"

"Hell . . . he lost beef, too! Maybe not as many as some of them others claim they did, but there was aplenty. Ten, twenty head regular like. Hurt bad."

"There much of a herd left now?"

"Five, six hundred head. Saul sold off a bunch of steers last year . . . six hundred. Market was good. Got eighteen dollars a piece for two-year-olds at Dalhart. That's where folks around here trail drive to. Takes about a week."

Ruskin made no comment. The ranch should be in good shape after Saul Gans had made such a deal. And with a herd of that size still grazing on the range, he'd have a fine start regardless of his neighbors' attitude.

"I'm hoping Rufe knowed what he was talking about."

Dave glanced at Link Henry, the words having no meaning for him. "Who?"

"Rufe . . . Rufe Hyatt. Said he had proof or something that'd clear up things around here. I'm hoping it's so. Country's like a powder keg. Going to blow sky high unless something's done mighty soon."

"I heard him mention it . . . didn't know what he was talking about at the time. You got any idea who's doing the rustling?"

Link wagged his head. "Must be some gang coming in from west of here . . . maybe holed up in the Sangre de Cristos." He pointed to the distant smudge of mountains beyond the low hills.

Ruskin considered that thoughtfully. Then: "You're pretty sure it couldn't be some of the hands working for my uncle . . . me? Seems to be a lot of people thinking that."

"Could be . . . sure. Could be 'most anybody. Only, how'd they get cattle moved through here without somebody spotting them? How'd they get them to Dalhart without Darrow or Trigg seeing them? Only way to the railroad is the trail between the two places, or across them, and you can't move even a little jag of critters without raising dust."

"Could use some other railhead."

"Only Denver, and that's a mighty mean trail. And there'd be no sense going right by Dalhart to reach Wichita or Dodge."

There was no arguing with that, Dave realized. A thought crossed his mind. "There a chance somebody's got a ranch close by where the rustlers could make their gather?"

"Been thought of, and nobody's ever found it if there is . . . and a lot of looking's been done. Only five ranches in the valley. You're setting about the middle. Pool's north of you, Hyatt's to the south. Darrow and Floyd Trigg are both east. Ain't hardly no ground left when you figure what's covered."

The buckboard rolled on steadily, now following a northwesterly course. Henry pointed to a fork leading to the left a short distance ahead.

"Goes to Hyatt's. Next turn off'll be to the right. Takes you to Trigg's."

"Road run all the way up the valley?"

"All the way. After we pass Trigg's, be a fork to the left again. Goes to Saul's . . . your place, I mean. On beyond that you come to a three-way split. One to the right leads to Darrow's, left to Amos Pool. Keep going straight and you'll end up in Colorado."

"What river's that?" Dave asked, pointing to a gleaming strip well to the west.

"The Tinaja. Busts into two creeks above Pool's. One fork cuts down through his spread and on to yours and Hyatt's. Other one swings east, takes care of Darrow and Trigg. The town, too."

"Pretty fair-sized stream."

Link nodded. "If it ever goes dry, this country's in big trouble. But I reckon it won't. Comes out of the Colorado mountains and there's always aplenty of snow there to fill it."

"How big a crew we got?"

Henry tugged at his trailing moustache, did some laborious calculating. "Counting old Nano, the cook, there's fourteen, I reckon."

"Fourteen," Dave echoed, astonished. "A hell of a lot of men for no more stock than we're running. Saul usually have a bigger herd?"

"No more'n a thousand, twelve hundred head, near as I can recollect."

"How long since he had that many?"

"Been a year."

"And he kept a full crew all the time since?"

Link shrugged his thin shoulders. "Well, they just sort of hung around. Suppose he paid them, but I don't know for sure. Always paid me."

"What about when Saul died . . . didn't any of them quit, move on?"

"Was a couple, maybe."

"And the rest just stayed, collected no wages."

"About the size of it. Guess they figured same as me and the regulars did. Somebody'd show up someday and take over . . . namely you."

"The regulars?"

"The Mex . . . Tibo Alveron. And Joe Ely and Cass Trimble,

old Nano . . . and me. We've been with Saul from the start, mostly."

That bit of information struck Dave Ruskin as odd. Cowhands worked for pay, and, when none was forthcoming, they generally moved on to greener pastures. But he was grateful to Link Henry for not doing so and told him as much.

The old rider grunted. "I'm too old to go knocking around, drifting from here to yonder. Anyhow, I don't know no other place. Same goes for Nano and the others. Saul give us a home so we just stayed put." He paused, looked closely at Dave. "You mean what you was saying about keeping the crew?"

Ruskin nodded. "Most of them anyway. But if I let some go, it won't be because Hyatt and the other ranchers want me to. It'll be because I don't need them."

Link clucked approvingly. "Sure the right way to look at it, but you got too much help. How you going to pick who's staying and who's going?"

"I can tell after I've met them all. And I'll be asking you for a little advice."

A broad grin cracked the old cowpuncher's weathered face. "Pleasure me to help all I can. Here's where we turn off. Post over there marks the southeast corner of your property. Me and Saul put it there a long time ago."

"You two were pretty close, seems like."

Henry bobbed his head. "We were friends," he said simply.

"I'm hoping you'll feel the same about me. The way things look I'm going to need. . . ."

The backrest of the buckboard's seat erupted suddenly in a shower of splinters. In that same fragment of time the flat *crack* of a rifle broke the hot stillness of the land. For a long breath Dave Ruskin and Henry sat frozen, and then the old cowpuncher hauled in on the reins and brought the team to a stop.

"Get down!" he yelled.

Dave was already leaving the buckboard, going off in a low, flat dive. A second shot echoed as he hit the ground, rolled in behind a clump of rabbit brush, and dragged out his pistol. On the opposite side of the vehicle Link was scrambling for the protection of a rocky mound.

Ruskin remained motionless, ears straining for some definite sound that would reveal the location of the bushwhacker. He wasn't certain but it seemed the shots had come from his right.

The minutes dragged by. Dave drew himself upright slowly. No shots challenged his appearance. Whoever it was had gone. A steady anger flowed through him. He holstered his weapon, dusted himself briefly, and climbed back onto the buckboard.

Link Henry settled beside him on the seat, took up the reins. "Expect there ain't no doubt in your mind now how folks feel about you. If you aim to stay alive, just keep remembering this here's a hate ranch you're taking over."

IV

"How far to the ranch?" Ruskin asked in a taut voice.

"Three miles, little less."

"Get there . . . fast."

Link glanced at Dave's set features, slapped at the team with the reins. The buckboard leaped ahead, swaying from the sudden start, stirring up clouds of dust as it got under way.

"You thinking the bushwhacker was somebody from your own ranch?"

"I intend to find out."

"Could've been anybody," Link said. "The ranchers wasn't too happy with the way things turned out back in town. Wouldn't be the first time a hired gun's been brought in to do some killing."

"That what you think?" Dave asked sharply.

"Well, don't hardly seem it'd be happening so soon."

"Which makes the odds good it was somebody from the ranch . . . one of my own crew."

"Does kind of narrow things down."

"And to shave it a little closer, which one wouldn't want me around to take over?"

Link shrugged. "Was I naming names, I'd say Jess Veetch. Was real put out when you popped up in the will. Figured Saul should've left him the place, and said as much. And then there's Cully Moss. Him and Jess is thicker'n cold grease. What Jess thinks, Cully thinks."

"Makes him a pretty good prospect," Dave said, looking ahead as they whirled up to the summit of a short rise. "That the ranch?"

"That's it."

Ruskin's eyes settled on the small cluster of buildings in a hollow near a stream. It was a barren, almost desolate-looking place, the severity of it broken only by a tiny grove of trees a short distance from the structures.

"Ain't much for show," Henry said, voicing his thoughts, "but it could be made into a mighty fine place. Saul never was no hand for being fancy. Wanted just what it took to raise cattle. You got something special in mind when we get there?"

"Head straight for the horses. I want to see which one's still warm."

The old cowpuncher nodded his understanding. "That'll be the main corral."

They sped past the main house where two men sat hunched on the porch, backs to the wall, smoking lazily. An elderly Mexican wearing a tattered, dirty apron peeled potatoes in the shade at the rear of the building. No one else was in sight.

Link guided the buckboard to the corral and pulled to a halt. A dozen horses, some of which were saddled, dozed in the streaming sunlight.

Dave dropped lightly to the ground, climbed the shaved poles, and lowered himself into the enclosure. Grim anger pushing at him relentlessly, he made a swift inspection of each horse. All were cool, showed no indication of having been ridden for hours. He returned to the buckboard.

"Not there. Anywhere else we ought to look? How about the barn?"

"Get in," Link said. "We'll make for certain."

Ruskin pulled himself onto the seat and a quick tour of the premises was made, ending up in the runway of the barn. No other horses were found.

"Reckon that settles that," the older man said, climbing from the vehicle. "Whoever it was didn't come back here."

"That's all it does prove," Dave answered, staring at the house. "Could've been somebody working the range."

"And it could've been a hired gun the ranchers had all set and waiting, just in case. Don't be forgetting that."

"Not forgetting anything," Ruskin said quietly, and picked up his blanket roll from the rear of the buckboard. "Where'll Veetch and the others be?"

"Up in the main house," Link said, and started for the door.

Dave fell in beside the old cowpuncher, his glance shifting back and forth as they struck across the wide yard. The place was in bad condition, he noted. Saul Gans's crew may have stayed on the job since his death but they had done little toward keeping things up.

The elderly Mexican was standing just outside the door of the kitchen when they reached the house. Link paused.

"This here's Nano, the cook."

Dave extended his hand. The dark, wrinkled face of the Mexican broke into a ragged-toothed smile.

"Buenos días," he murmured politely. *"¿Como está usted?"*

"Muy bien, gracias," Ruskin replied.

The man's grin widened and he bowed deeply as they moved on. Coming to the rear entrance of the building, Henry jerked open the dust-clogged screen, stepped inside. The place was stuffy, uncomfortable with trapped heat. Somewhere in the front Dave could hear the low mutter of voices.

"Still at it," Henry said, and, taking Ruskin's blanket roll from him, tossed it into a dust-covered chair and led the way down a narrow hall to a large room that extended the full width of the house.

A half dozen men were present, one sleeping on a couch against the south wall, the remainder gathered around a table upon which were cards, piles of silver coins, glasses, and a half-filled whiskey bottle. Several empty bottles, souvenirs of previous games, had been thrown into the sooty fireplace.

All looked up indolently as Ruskin and Link entered. One, a thick-bodied, coarse-featured man, turned and, without rising, thrust out his hand.

"Expect you're Ruskin. I'm Jess Veetch."

Dave took the ramrod's fingers into his own. Sharp words were on his lips but he held them back, waited.

Veetch nodded at the man to his right. "Pete Anson," he said, and then continued on around the table. "Art Nabors, Jude Wilson, Hank Baker. Jasper doing the sleeping there is Tom Gries. Boys, this here's your new boss, Mister Ruskin."

Dave touched each with a cool look, brought his attention back to Veetch. "This usual . . . crew hanging around the house in the middle of the day?"

The foreman stirred lazily. "Why not? They been doing night-hawking. Wasn't sleepy so we got to playing cards. Got four men looking after the stock."

"With all this rustling going on you've got just four riders taking care of six hundred head?"

"That's aplenty . . . and there ain't six hundred head. About half that."

"What happened to the rest?" Link Henry broke in.

Veetch turned his head slowly, stared at Link. "What rest? Three hundred's all we had, old man. You don't know nothing about it."

"Know enough to count," Henry said. "Was a good six hundred left after Saul sold off that bunch last year."

"You just think there was," the foreman said in that same level tone. Abruptly he tossed his cards onto the table, rose, faced Dave. "What's he been telling you, Ruskin?"

Dislike for Veetch had been immediate. Clinging to his temper, Dave wheeled, crossed the room to where the sleeping Tom Gries still snored deeply.

"Not enough, I'd guess," he said, and, taking the back of the couch in his hands, he tipped it forward, dumped the cowpuncher onto the floor. Gries came up fast, eyes flaring.

"What the hell . . . ?"

"Do your sleeping in the bunkhouse," Ruskin snapped, and returned to the table. "Goes for this, too," he added, pointing at the cards. "I'm not against poker playing, but you won't be doing it in here and on my time. Understand?"

Veetch's eyes narrowed, and then he smiled faintly. "Why, sure, Mister Ruskin. You're the boss. Get up, boys . . . move your duds to the bunkhouse. We ain't welcome here no more."

Faces stolid, the men at the table pulled back, the surliness in their attitudes plain. Silently Dave watched them move out. Then he glanced around.

"Want this place cleaned up. Worse than a hog pen. Send whoever. . . ."

"Won't be one of them doing it," Veetch cut in. "They're cowhands. Reckon you'll have to hire yourself a handyman.

Maybe you could use Link there. Ain't no good for nothing else."

"Few more around here I could name that's in the same fix," Henry said angrily.

"You figuring on making some changes in the crew, Mister Ruskin?" Veetch continued, completely ignoring Link.

"Coming to that later. Want to meet them all at suppertime. You can spell off the men night-hawking long enough for me to meet them."

Jess Veetch nodded. "Just whatever you say, Mister Ruskin," he said, and left the house by the front door.

The sarcasm in the man's tone bit deeply into Dave Ruskin, and the closely guarded anger within him surged to the fore. He'd like nothing better than to overtake Veetch and. . . .

"Night-hawking!"

Link Henry's voice jarred him to awareness.

"Only night-hawking that bunch has ever done was at Fred Banner's saloon!"

Dave turned to the old man. "You mean nobody rides herd at night?"

"None of them, and that's a fact. Me and the Mex. We sort of trade off with Ely and Cass Trimble. Once in a while Jess and maybe Cully Moss'll ride by, have themselves a look. Mostly you'll find them doing what you seen here today."

Dave's thoughts had come to a stop. "Cully Moss. You talked about him before. Where was he?"

Link scratched at his chin. "Come to think of it, he sure ain't around. Kind of funny."

"Veetch said he had four men with the herd. Three of them will be the ones you named. Think he's the fourth?"

"Ain't likely. Reckon nobody ever caught Cully doing any work." Henry paused, turned his shrewd old eyes to Dave. "You thinking what I am?"

"Expect so . . . and I aim to find out for sure in the next couple of days."

After the evening meal was over and the six men Dave had insisted ride night herd had gone, he sat alone at the table, drinking Nano's strong, black coffee.

It appeared to him that only Link Henry and the men mentioned favorably by the old cowpuncher were sincerely interested in the ranch and in doing a day's work for him.

Perhaps, during the time when Saul Gans was alive and running things, Veetch and the others were of value, but that had all changed. He should blame the foreman for that, he supposed. Veetch should have kept them on the job, forced them either to work or move on. They now had a strange attitude toward things—one that he didn't like.

This was particularly true of Cully Moss, a slightly built, young blond with small, sharp eyes. As with Veetch, he had disliked the rider instantly, but as also in the case of the foreman he endeavored to put his personal feelings aside, judge the man fairly on merit. But it was no use. He could see nothing in Cully Moss that was worth consideration.

As for his suspicions, he failed completely to tie the young rider in with the bushwhacker. Alveron, the *vaquero,* had seen Cully on the range working the herd. It was strange, he said, but Cully was there. The fact far from satisfied Dave but he had no choice other than to let matters ride, keep his eyes open.

He was forced to do something about the crew—reduce it by half at least. He could figure on Link, the *vaquero,* Cass Trimble, and Joe Ely. He'd need at least two more, not counting Nano, the cook. Later, when he got the herd built up some, he could add more.

The herd—who was wrong in the count? If Link Henry was right, 300 head had disappeared since Saul Gans died. If they had been rustled, Veetch certainly would have said so. Could the old cowpuncher be wrong? That he hated the foreman and the men who hung around him was apparent, and accordingly could be expected to have little good to say for him.

Ruskin shook his head. There were too many unanswered questions, but after all it was just the first day, he thought. He couldn't expect to understand and settle all his problems so soon. He'd make a trip to town in the morning, pay a call on the banker, establish his claim, and see where he stood insofar as cash was concerned. Then he'd know what his next move would be.

V

It was the finest hour of the day. The sun had just begun its climb into a sky streaked with wisps of clouds, and the long draws and graceful slopes had yet to surrender the coolness stored during the night to the driving heat when Dave Ruskin turned into the road that led to Apache Wells. Astride a tall bay selected from the remuda, he looked over the still shadowy land, felt a stir of pride. This was all his—a ranch of his own, a dream he thought could never come true. But it had, and regardless of the troubles he faced, he'd never give it up.

He swung from the marked trail at this point, grinned as a long-eared jack rabbit spurted from under the bay's hoofs, loped off in easy bounds through the snakeweed dotting the swale into which he rode. He had chosen to ignore the usual route earlier, preferring to cut across country for a better look at his holdings. But the idea had been Link Henry's, also. The old cowpuncher had been thinking about the hidden rifleman, Dave knew, but said nothing about it, simply placed it as a suggestion. He had smiled at Henry and agreed. The possibility of a second attempt on his life was very real and it would be smart to take precautions, stay alert. Link had wanted to accompany him into town to see Aaron Powell, the banker, but he had refused that offer. He felt it was a good idea to have Henry on hand at the ranch when he was absent.

He had company, nevertheless. Fleeting motion farther to the right of the departing jack rabbit brought him to sudden attention. It was only a faint blur, like a shifting shadow, somewhere in a deep wash that ran parallel to the hollow he was crossing, but it was there.

Slowing the bay, he settled back on the saddle, moved his holstered gun forward on his leg to where it would be quickly available. Continuing on until he reached a hill of fair size, he veered from course, circled the rise, and came into the arroyo at right angles. The rider he had seen broke from the brush at almost the same instant, halted abruptly.

Tibo Alveron, the *vaquero.*

Hand resting on his pistol, Dave contained his surprise and studied the man coldly.

"Good way to stop a bullet, *amigo.*"

Alveron, a slim, dark-faced man with quiet eyes and a soft voice, shrugged slightly. The preceding evening Dave had met and liked the *vaquero,* but now he was having doubts.

"You are not the greenhorn the *viejo* feared, *señor,*" Alveron murmured.

Ruskin's shoulders relaxed. A half smile crossed his lips. "Link sent you to look after me, that it?"

Tibo laid his hands on the broad horn of his ornate Mexican saddle. "He told me of the ambush. It could again happen. I was to watch, take care."

Dave shook his head, vaguely angered. "Expect I can look after myself. Been doing it for quite a spell."

Alveron shrugged again in the ancient way of his people. "It is true. But in this country a man needs a friend. I am that, *señor.*"

Ruskin considered that simple truth. After a moment he said: "Good enough . . . but we ride together. Let's go."

They continued on, little passing between them but an occasional comment. He was pleased that he had been right about the Mexican, chided himself for that one moment of doubt when he discovered the *vaquero* was riding his trail. The coolness and respect with which Veetch and his followers treated the man should have been proof enough.

Reaching the settlement, they rode shoulder to shoulder down the center of the street, and halted at the hitch rack fronting the bank. Both dismounted, and Alveron, drawing his sack of tobacco and brown papers from a pocket, leaned against the building.

"I will be here, *señor*," he said laconically as Dave opened the door.

Aaron Powell greeted him with a lifeless handshake and thumbed through the papers Dave had been instructed to give him. After comparing them with others removed from an envelope, the banker nodded.

"You're the heir, all right. What can I do for you?"

Ruskin tucked the papers back into his pocket. "Like to know where I stand. Ranch is in bad shape and it'll take cash to fix it. How much money do I have?"

Powell shook his head. "None."

"None?" Dave echoed. "You sure of that?"

"Of course I'm sure," the banker said stiffly. "Saul Gans didn't believe in banks. Kept his money home. If he had any, that's where you'll find it."

There had been none in his uncle's desk. Dave had spent hours that previous night going through papers, learning all he could about the operation of the ranch. There had been no sign of cash.

"Fact is," Powell said, "it's the other way around. I'm holding a mortgage on Saul's . . . your place. Twenty-five hundred dollars."

A new wave of disappointment rolled through Dave. "Past due?"

"Will be in ninety days. A thousand's due then."

Ninety days. Ruskin stirred wearily. It would be difficult to raise $1,000 in that length of time, considering all else.

"Saul was behind, but he caught up all his back payments and interest last summer when he sold part of his herd."

"How much did that come to?"

The banker pursed his lips. "About three thousand, I recall."

"Then what happened to the rest of the money? I understand he sold off six hundred head, got better than ten dollars a head for the lot."

"How would I know?" Powell said, nettled. "He paid me, and I expect he had quite a few other bills around town. Owed Yates a big sum. Had a feed bill at Washburn's."

Dave stared through the window into the street. Harvey Drace, star glinting in the sunlight, was moving slowly along the walk on the opposite side.

"Ten thousand is a lot of money."

"Imagine he used it to square things up. Heard once he had a woman in Denver. Made a trip up there now and then. That could account for a lot of it."

"I suppose it could," Dave said. "The point is, it leaves me about broke. My credit good for a loan?"

Aaron Powell turned to his desk, began to shuffle papers. "Right now, I'm afraid there's nothing I can do for you. One mortgage on the place is all I can handle. You get things going right. . . ."

"Sure," Ruskin cut in angrily. "When I don't need it, you're willing to help."

"The bank can't afford to take chances. Not good business."

Dave sighed. He could understand Powell, guessed he wasn't a very good risk at that moment. But that would change.

"One thing I'd like that won't cost you anything."

The banker's brows lifted. "Yes?"

"Some information. My uncle ever mention to you how big a herd he had?"

Powell again pursed his lips. "Matter of fact, he did say something about it last year when he was getting ready for the drive. Told me he was selling off half of what he had."

Dave nodded slowly. Link Henry had been right. There should be somewhere between 500 and 600 steers on the range—not the lesser number that Jess Veetch claimed.

Turning, he started for the door. Powell's voice checked him.

"That mortgage payment . . . ninety days. You think you'll be able to make it?"

"I'll make it," Ruskin said, and moved on.

The sooner he got back to the ranch, confronted Veetch, the quicker he'd get to the bottom of things.

VI

"Fact is," Dave Ruskin said in a carefully controlled voice, "we had close to six hundred steers left after the sale last summer. Got that from some reliable people. You claim there's less than half that many on the range. What happened to the rest?"

Jess Veetch leaned against the side of the bunkhouse, thumbs hooked in his belt, and glanced in sly amusement at the men gathered around him. He grinned at Dave.

"You accusing me of rustling?"

"Not accusing anybody of anything. Just looking for some answers . . . and you, being the ramrod of this outfit, ought to have them."

"You're damn' right I do!" Veetch said, all humor vanishing suddenly. "Now, get this straight . . . there never was no six hundred head. Don't make no difference what you been told."

"Rustlers got a few," Cully Moss volunteered.

Veetch bobbed his head. "There was plenty didn't make it through the winter, too. Snow always kills off a bunch."

"Two hundred or more?"

"Could be. I don't know . . . but there sure wasn't no six hundred."

Ruskin swore in disgust. He was getting nowhere. Half the cattle Saul Gans had on the range after his sale at Dalhart had disappeared. Nobody, the foreman least of all, could furnish any explanation. One thing however had become clear to Dave. Jess Veetch's time as a foreman was finished. He was through, along with Moss and all the others who felt as he did.

"Saul Gans got better than ten thousand dollars at that sale last year. I've run down about half that, paid out to the bank and on debts. Any idea where the rest of it is?"

Veetch's jaw tightened and his features settled into hard lines. "You saying I had something to do with it?"

Dave shrugged. Behind him Tibo Alveron shifted slightly to one side, his small, black eyes sharp and watchful. Beyond, at the door of the house, Link Henry made a small noise as he changed his position from one foot to another.

"You were his foreman," Ruskin said. "Closest man to him. If anybody'd know, it would be you."

"Well, I sure'n hell don't. What the old man done with his money was his business. I don't know nothing about that, and I don't know nothing about them steers you claim's missing. That what you want me to say?"

Dave studied the man's withdrawn features for several moments. "That's what I expected you to say. Just wanted to hear it."

"All right, then. What's next on your mind?"

"You're fired," Ruskin said flatly.

The statement was so bald, so unexpected, that Veetch's eyes flew open and his jaw sagged. He stared blankly at Dave, turned then to look at Cully Moss and the others siding him. "What's that?"

"You heard it. Can't afford your kind working for me."

"You got to have somebody. Who . . . ?"

"Be none of your friends," Dave said coolly. "Men I'm keeping have already been told. You've got thirty minutes to get your gear together and move out."

Cully Moss tugged at his hat. "How about the back wages owed us?"

"You'll get paid, even if you didn't earn any. It'll take a little time. Thanks to you, I'm about flat broke. Drop by the bank and tell Powell where you'll be. He'll send you the money when I raise it."

"Maybe I don't want to wait."

"Suit yourself. The way I see it, you've got no choice. Nobody asked you to hang around here after Saul Gans died."

"Somebody had to," Jess Veetch declared. "Place would've gone to hell."

"Seems it did, anyway," Dave broke in dryly. "If it hadn't been for Link and Alveron, couple others, I doubt if there'd been anything left."

Veetch rocked back on his heels, a satisfied look on his face. "So that's the how of it! The old man and the Mex. Might've known, the way they been sneaking around, spying. . . ."

"You've wasted five minutes of your thirty," Ruskin said.

"The hell with you and your thirty minutes!" the foreman exploded suddenly. "I don't have to pull out! Place is more mine than yours, anyway, and no four-flushing bastard of a johnny-come-lately. . . ."

Ruskin hit him, hard and clean, on the point of the jaw. Veetch staggered back, flung out his arms to keep from falling. He clutched the shoulder of the man standing directly behind him, righted himself, lunged forward.

Dave side-stepped quickly, drove a second blow to Veetch's head as he stumbled by, sent him to his knees. Instantly Cully Moss swung around, dropped into a crouch. Tibo Alveron's quiet voice froze him.

"No, *amigo* . . . if you would live."

Moss straightened slowly, stepped back as Veetch pulled himself upright groggily.

"Get out," Ruskin said in a cold voice. "All of you! If I catch any of you on my land again . . . have a gun in your hand."

"Big talk. Enough of us here to take this place apart, board by board," Cully said derisively.

"Look around," Ruskin suggested quietly. "Then make up your mind."

Cully frowned, swung his gaze in a slow circle, his glance touching Joe Ely in the doorway of the barn loft, Cass Trimble at the opposite end of the bunkhouse. Both had rifles. Link Henry had now stepped deeper into the yard, a shotgun cradled in his long arms. Alveron's hands were hanging at his sides, hovering above the twin pistols he wore.

"Up to you. Make it easy or make it hard," Dave said.

"Forget it, Cully," Veetch said irritably. "Ain't worth it. Whole damned ranch ain't worth it."

"Not to you, maybe," Ruskin replied. "It is to me. That's what makes up the difference."

Veetch spat, threw a glance at Moss and the others. "Come on, let's get out of here," he said.

Cully made no move, but continued to stare at Dave. "Ain't ready. Little something I'd like to settle. . . ."

"Don't be a fool!" Veetch snarled. "They'd blow you in two first move you make."

"Let him try." Ruskin's voice was dry as winter leaves. Cully continued to stare, then abruptly he turned away, and fell in with the others.

As Dave, flanked now by his entire crew, watched them go, the thought twisted wryly through him that he now had not only all of Fire Valley's ranchers against him but his one-time foreman and crew as well.

"Reckon you know this ain't ending here," Link said.

"Don't expect it will," Ruskin answered, "but a man's got to start somewhere driving out the snakes."

"Jess was lying about them missing steers . . . and that money, too."

"I know that, but there's not much I can do about it now. Best thing's to forget it, start over." He turned to Alveron. "Tibo, take Joe and Cass and cut out a hundred steers."

The *vaquero*'s brows lifted. "We make a drive to Dalhart?"

"Only thing I can do. Hate selling any of the stock, but we need cash. Credit's no good anywhere . . . not even for grub . . . and you men have to be paid. The only answer is to sell part of the herd."

"Far as wages are concerned," Joe Ely said, "I ain't hurting none for mine. Was I to get paid, I'd just blow it down at Banner's place."

"Expect we all feel that way," Link said. "Don't go fretting none over that part of it."

Dave smiled. "I appreciate that, and I'm obliged. But I've got to raise some cash . . . working capital they call it. Then we can start putting this ranch back in shape."

Alveron nodded. "We start the drive when, *señor?*"

"Tomorrow, if we can make it."

"The *brutos* will be ready," the *vaquero* said.

VII

The drive shaped up quickly. Deciding not to take the cook wagon, Dave had Nano accumulate sufficient food to get them through the week and had it stowed on a pack horse. The cook and Cass Trimble were to remain on the ranch, look after it and the remaining cattle during the absence of the others.

It was a hamstrung operation, he knew, four men making a drive, two left to guard the balance of the herd. Earlier he had considered leaving either Link Henry or Joe Ely behind, also, but later he ruled out the idea; getting the herd to Dalhart safely and quickly was of utmost importance.

With an extra mount each, they headed out near the middle of the afternoon, pointing due east. They'd not get far before sundown but at least the drive would be under way and the herd leader would have found his place at the front of the column.

They halted at dark only a few miles from the ranch, and, as the herd flowed down into a shallow basin for the night's rest, Dave waved his riders in.

"Need to keep a sharp watch," he said. "Don't know whether we'll have trouble with Veetch and his crowd or not. I doubt it, as I don't think they're expecting us to move so soon. Best we be on guard, however."

"Might as well expect it," Link said dourly. "That Jess, smarting like he is, won't let things ride."

"Set up camp here on this high spot. There'll be some moon tonight and it won't be too hard to see. We ride herd in four-hour shifts. Tibo, you and Joe take the first one. Link and I'll throw some grub together, holler you in when it's ready."

It worked out well and the night passed with no interruptions. By daylight the herd was on the move again under a cloudy sky that gave promise of relief from the blistering heat.

"Is there only one trail to the railhead?" he asked the old

cowpuncher as they moved on at a good pace. "We need to reach Dalhart and get back to the ranch fast as we can. If you know a short cut, let's take it."

Henry wagged his head. "Ain't but one way . . . through Indian Gulch. Lays about the middle betwixt the Darrow and the Trigg places. Once we're out of there, we'll be up on the flats, and Dalhart'll be straight east."

"When's the next water?"

"Be late tomorrow. Mestizo Creek, comes off the east fork of the Tinaja. Place called the Red Bluffs where we cross. Hit the Tinaja day after that."

"And then no more water until we reach Dalhart?"

"That's the way it'll be, but the cattle'll do fine. Never have no trouble."

They made excellent time that day, and the next morning the herd was up and moving without persuasion.

Joe Ely rode up, paused beside Dave. "We keep having this kind of luck we'll be in Dalhart 'most 'fore we know it!"

Link Henry grinned, added: "Weather like this sure makes trail driving a pure pleasure."

Dave hoped it would continue but he had doubts. Once they were beyond the last water source, crossing the vast Apache Plain, it wouldn't be so easy. That was a lesser worry, however; it was the possibility of trouble from Jess Veetch and his bunch that disturbed him. With only three riders he'd have small chance of standing off a raid.

He wished there was some way he could prove the hunch that persistently plagued his mind—that Veetch had somehow gotten his hands on the money—but there was nothing to go on. Link Henry, who had been closest to Saul, could give him no help on the matter.

"Saul owed a powerful lot of folks," the old rider said. "Reckon he paid them all off, though."

Dave had recalled something the banker had mentioned. "This woman in Denver . . . could he have given it to her?"

Henry looked at him in surprise. "How'd you know about her?"

"Powell told me."

"Well, wasn't like Aaron's making out. She was the wife of a friend Saul had. Was mighty sick in a hospital or some such place as that. The friend had got hisself jailed for life and Saul was sort of looking after her."

"That could run into money . . . a lot of it."

"Expect it did, only she died a couple of years back. None of that cash you're looking for went to her."

That had cleared up one possibility. "You've never come right out and said whether you think Veetch could have somehow grabbed it or not."

"Mostly because I plain don't know. Jess would have had plenty of chances, that's for sure. He was the one who found Saul when he died."

"I've been meaning to ask about that. How'd it happen?"

"He was riding in that rough country, south of the ranch. Looking for strays, I expect. Something spooked his horse. Hit his head on a rock when he landed. Dead real sudden."

"Veetch was with him?"

"Nope. Him and Cully was working the south fence. Seen Saul's horse trotting for home. Backtracked and found the old man."

Dave considered that, then asked: "Was that when Veetch sort of moved in, took over?"

"If you're meaning him starting to live in the main house, fool around Saul's desk and such, it was. Told him myself he had no business doing it."

"What did he say?"

"That I'd best keep my nose out of things, and if I didn't like it to pull freight. Somebody had to look after things until the lawyers got things settled, he said."

There, perhaps, was the answer, Dave realized. Gans could have kept his surplus cash in the desk. Veetch could have discovered it, taken possession—and there'd be no way of proving any of it. He might as well forget the missing money, concentrate on building up the ranch by his own efforts. But, after all was said and done, Veetch could be innocent. There were dozens of things Gans could have done with his money. Ruskin could prove nothing.

They reached Mestizo Creek, a wide, shallow stream that cut a path through a steep-walled channel a short distance from a line of ragged bluffs, just at dusk. They halted the herd in a grassy swale near the crossing, made camp not far away.

The usual four-hour shift was maintained, with Dave and Link Henry taking the initial stint this time.

Shortly before midnight Ely and Alveron relieved them. Dave, worn out by the long day's riding, poured himself a last cup of coffee and was moving to where his blanket roll lay, when a distant sound brought him up in mid-stride.

He glanced at Henry, wondering if the old man had also heard, but Link was already asleep, snoring deeply. Ruskin turned then, cocked his ear into the night. It had sounded like a yell—one of surprise. A coyote, he decided finally when it did not come again. Gulping the last of his coffee, he tossed the cup aside and dropped wearily onto his blankets.

A moment later he was on his feet once more, brought upright by a sudden spatter of gunshots.

VIII

The night came alive with yells, the *pound* of hoofs, the *crackling* of guns. Dave, pistol in hand, wheeled, started for his horse. Abruptly two riders loomed before him, racing out of the half dark. Dave threw himself to the left, barely escaped being run down.

Pistols flashed at close range, blinding him. Bullets *thudded* into the ground near his head. Rolling frantically, he tried to find cover, bring his own weapon into use.

"Dave! Dave!"

It was Link Henry's anxious voice. The old cowpuncher was somewhere off to the right. More yelling was coming from the swale where the herd had bedded, and steers were bawling noisily, the sound punctuated by continuing gunshots.

The two riders had wheeled, were returning. Anger swept through Ruskin in a hot burst. He crouched, fired hurriedly—missed. The horses were upon him suddenly, heaving dark shapes in the night. He triggered his weapon again, heard a man curse. And then a powerful force struck him on the side of the head.

His senses reeled. He slammed to the ground with sickening impact. Pain roared through him and a vast, black silence overwhelmed him.

He became aware of motion, fought to clear the cobwebs from his numbed brain. He was being dragged. As if from a great distance Link Henry's voice penetrated his consciousness.

"Help me, boy . . . help me. Can't do it alone. You got to crawl . . . help."

Obediently, woodenly, Dave began to work his legs, use his arms. They seemed detached from the rest of his body.

A strong hand gripped his shirt collar, was pulling him steadily on. He made out the shape of Link. The older man was ahead of him, on his knees. There seemed to be more shooting than before; that fact registered dully on his mind. He swallowed hard, broke the dryness of his throat, found his voice.

"What . . . ?"

"Just keep crawling," Henry's voice said. "Got to make it to them bluffs . . . hide. Ain't far now."

Ruskin halted, tried to rise, the driving power of anger having its way with him.

"Stay down!" Link rasped hoarsely, and pulled him back. "Bastards are all over the place!"

Ruskin sprawled on the cool sand. "Let me be!" he snarled. "I'm not letting them. . . ."

"You're doing what I tell you. Get yourself killed for sure, raising up like that."

Three riders swept by in a thunder of hoofs little more than a wagon's length away. Flat on the ground, shielded only by a thin stand of weeds, Dave watched their shadowy passage.

"Hunting for us," Link muttered.

Ruskin's mind was finally beginning to clear. "Who?"

"Can't tell. Wearing masks. Come on . . . we better find cover quick."

Henry moved on. Dave followed. He was finding it difficult to concentrate, organize his thoughts. Things would flash through his mind, hang briefly, and fade out. They'd been raided—that fact stuck with him. There were a lot of riders, a great deal of shooting.

"Here we are," he heard Link say.

Ruskin lifted his bead slightly, weathered a gust of pain the effort induced, saw they were at the foot of the bluffs. Thick brush was all around them, and all was cloaked with shadow.

The gunfire was continuing, seemingly heavier now near the creek, and in his befuddled state Dave wondered at that. Farther to the left was another pocket of steady shooting.

"Here . . . let me have a look at you."

Dave felt Henry pull him around, tip his face to the feeble moonlight filtering over the rim of the bluff above them. Fingers pressed against the side of his head. He winced.

"Got yourself a dinger of a wallop," the old cowpuncher said. "Hoof, most likely . . . when that pair rode you down. Just lay back. Little resting'll fix you up."

Things were beginning to clarify, make sense. Two of the outlaws had tried to drive him into the ground, missed on their first try, caught him on the second. He'd taken a blow to the head, lost consciousness—and all the while other outlaws were driving off his herd.

"Damn them!" he blurted suddenly, pulling himself to a sitting position.

"Hush," Link Henry hissed. "Couple of them coming. Still looking for us."

Dave's hand dropped to his holster. "They'll find us," he promised, and then the words died on his lips as his fingers touched the empty leather on his hip. He'd lost his weapon, probably when he'd gone down. He turned hurriedly to Henry.

"Your gun . . . give it to me."

"Ain't got it. Back there . . . in my blankets."

Ruskin swore in frustrated rage, crouched lower in the brush, and watched the two outlaws move by slowly. "One's dead . . . swear to that," a voice said.

"Then where the hell is he?" another demanded impatiently. "Ain't no dead man getting up and walking away!"

"Other 'n' must have lugged him off somewheres."

The words faded as the men passed on. Tense, muscles trembling with helpless fury, Dave stared after them. "Know who they are?"

"Couldn't tell. Them masks. . . ."

"The voices. Weren't they familiar?"

"Sounded mushy like. Don't recollect hearing them before. Could've been them masks doing it."

Ruskin lay back, favoring his throbbing head. He could do nothing, could only hide, wait until the marauders had gone.

But then things would change. He'd recover his weapon, get his horse—and follow. A herd of cattle wouldn't be hard to track. And the outlaws had made a big mistake. Apparently their plan had been to kill him, along with Link and Tibo and Joe Ely, so that there'd be no survivors. Tibo and Joe. His thoughts paused there. Where were they? He sat up again, glanced at Henry.

"See any sign of the others?"

"Joe and the Mex? Nope. Was a right smart of shooting going on up above us. Expect that was them. Been quiet there the last few minutes."

Dave settled back again.

Link gave him a sidewise look. "Ain't no use fretting. We're caught right here till they pull out . . . and that ain't going to be until they're sure we're dead, or maybe daylight comes. Best you be resting that head of yours."

Dave stirred. "Getting Tibo and Joe killed. . . . Herd wasn't worth it. Nothing is."

"Now, we don't know they're dead. Could've got themselves holed up, same as us. And don't go blaming yourself if they run into some bad luck. They're growed men, both of them."

"A hundred stinking steers," Ruskin said savagely. "Not worth it. Ten times a hundred wouldn't be worth it!"

"Man's got a right to fight for what's his. Don't make no difference what it's worth. Careful. Here they come again."

Dave turned, watched the outlaws—three of them this time—ride by slowly, dark, silent silhouettes in the night. It was quiet. The shooting had stopped, but the search was continuing. He felt suddenly very tired and the pain in his head had settled into a dull, deep throbbing. He closed his eyes. . . .

IX

Ruskin awoke suddenly. For a long minute he lay perfectly quiet, feeling the bite of the morning chill, the sullen ache in his head where the horse's hoof had struck its glancing blow. And then as realization came to him, he sat up.

Link Henry was sitting close by, thin shoulders hunched, head thrust forward. He was staring into the half dark toward the creek. Beyond, a faint pearl was spreading above the eastern horizon.

"How long've I been sleeping?" Dave asked irritably.

"Four, maybe five hours. Feeling better, ain't you?"

"Some," Ruskin admitted grudgingly. It angered him to think of the time lost while he slept, but a moment later the sobering thought came to him that awake or not there was nothing he could have done.

"They still out there?"

"Ain't sure. Seen something moving a while back. One thing's certain . . . the herd's gone."

Dave shifted his attention to the small hollow where the cattle had halted. Even in the poor light he could see that it was deserted.

"They won't get far," he said in a low voice. "I aim to start trailing soon as it's light enough."

"On foot?"

Dave frowned. "Horses gone, too?"

"Ain't seen any."

Ruskin swore, and then faint hope lifted within him. "Could've just strayed down to the creek, or maybe crossed over. All that shooting would've spooked them."

Link only grunted, indicative of his doubts.

The minutes dragged by. The hint of light in the east brightened gradually, changed to flaring fingers of yellow.

"Looks like the Mex," Link said suddenly, and pulled himself to his feet.

Dave came up hurriedly, ignoring the wave of nausea that swept through him, looked in the direction the old cowpuncher indicated. A quarter mile above them a figure was moving out of the brush at the foot of the bluffs.

"He's all right," Ruskin said. "Where's Joe?"

"Ain't no sign of him yet."

Dave stepped out into the open, started down the slight grade for the creek. "Tibo's looking for us. Better get out where he can see us."

"Watch sharp," Henry warned, following. "Could be a couple of them bushwhacking bastards laying out there somewheres, waiting for us to show up."

"If I can find my gun, I'll be hoping there are," Dave replied. He turned, again looked toward the *vaquero.* Raising his arm, he waved. Alveron made an answering signal.

Pushed now by an urgent need to begin the search for the herd, Ruskin hurried to where their camp had been. Blankets, supplies, and all else lay scattered about. Muttering a curse, he moved to where he had encountered the two riders. After a few moments he found his pistol, half buried in the sand where he had lost it.

Brushing away the loose grit, he tested its action, then reloaded from the cartridges in his belt. Feeling better with the weight of the weapon resting against his leg, he walked on down to the edge of the embankment that overlooked the creek. There were no horses there, nor were there any on the flat beyond. Dave shrugged wearily. The outlaws had taken not only the herd but all the riding stock as well, leaving them stranded. He started back up the slope.

Link Henry had recovered his weapon, was now cutting away to meet the *vaquero.* Alveron was walking slowly. Dark stains showed on his left arm, again on the low side of his shirt. Ruskin quickened his step.

Tibo greeted him with a worn smile. "It is good to see you, *señor.* I feared for you and the old one."

"We hid out," Link said, coming up. "Where's Joe?"

The *vaquero* shook his head, pointed into the distance. "He is there . . . dead. A bullet from the back." The Mexican paused, looked squarely at Dave. "I am sorry. They come when we not see them. We did not expect. . . ."

"Forget it," Ruskin said. "Caught us all. You hurt bad?"

"Only scratches. It is nothing. Joe was not lucky."

"How'd you get away from them?" Henry asked.

"I run for the bluffs after Joe is shot. They chase me. When a bullet hits me, I fall, play like one dead. They think they have kill me, also . . . but I fool them."

"Dave, here, got a right smart clout to the head. Couple of them tried to ride him down. See anybody you know?"

Alveron shook his head. "All have covers on the face. The horses wear no brand."

"Must be the bunch who've been doing the rustling around here," Dave said. "Looks like they've got a regular system . . . masks, unbranded horses, and so on."

"The same, sure enough," Henry agreed. He turned again to the Mexican. "See any of our horses up your way?"

"No, they are gone, also. I saw two of the *ladrónes* drive them to the stream."

"Then we're flat afoot," Link groaned. He swore deeply. "Ain't nothing lower than a man leaving another one afoot in this country!"

Dave remained thoughtful for several moments, and then dropped back to the water. Link and Tibo followed, the latter squatting in the shallows to cleanse his wounds. They were superficial, the one in his side being no more than a bullet graze, the other, in his arm, similar but somewhat deeper.

Ruskin, glancing back, located the tracks of the herd leading down into the creek from the swale, and then waded on through the ankle-deep water to the opposite side. He was frowning.

There were no hoof marks on the slope where they had crossed.

He puzzled over that briefly, realized then that the outlaws had driven the steers through the water, thus wiping out all evidence of passage as well as keeping them out of sight in the channel. But they couldn't conceal the herd indefinitely; eventually they'd break out onto dry land. The question was, however, which direction had the outlaws taken? Upstream or down?

Dave's spirits fell. There was no way of knowing, and during the several hours the rustlers had kept him and the others of his crew pinned down, a considerable distance would have been covered.

Link Henry splashed across the creek, halted beside him. "Left us in a hell of a picklement, didn't they? Ain't no way of chasing a herd through water."

Dave nodded. "No signs left." The rustlers were taking no chances on revealing their location. Had the outlaws been certain all four of them were dead, he realized, they would not have bothered to use such care. Now, unsure, they were taking all precautions.

"Could be ten miles in either direction . . . upstream or downstream." Dave paused. "If they were heading out for Dalhart, which way would they take?"

"Wouldn't make no difference. Same distance. Could go north a spell, turn east . . . or they could go south. All comes out at the right place."

The *vaquero* had washed his wounds, and now had a bandage, improvised from strips of a bandanna, wrapped around his arm.

"With no horse there is little we can do."

Dave agreed. Mounted, they could separate, check both up and down the creek. The outlaws had realized that, too, and made it an impossibility. Impatient, he swung his glance in a circle.

"About where are we? Where's the nearest ranch we can get

something to ride?"

Link Henry glanced about. "Expect we're about the middle, betwixt Darrow's and Trigg's. A mite closer to Darrow, maybe."

"How far?"

"Take all day, walking."

"Guess we don't have much choice there." Dave turned to Alveron. "Where's Joe laying? Ought to bury him before we pull out."

The *vaquero* pointed toward the bluffs. "That way. I will show you."

Joe Ely was face down in the sand, one arm thrown across a clump of snakeweed, the other doubled beneath him. There were three bullet wounds in his back.

"They come from there," Alveron said, waving to a swale near the creek. "They hid there, I think, wait for us."

"Must have ridden in late," Dave said. "I remember crossing that bottom several times when we were bedding down the herd. Nobody was there then."

"Held off until only a couple of us was awake," Henry said. He looked down at Ely. "What'll we do with him? Ain't got nothing to dig with."

Ruskin pointed to the nearby bluffs. "Carry him over there, find a place where we can cave dirt down over him."

Finding a slight overhang, they placed Ely well back under it, and then, using their feet and a stick that Alveron found close by, they dislodged enough of the loose sand and clay to cover the dead man. As a further protection against wild animals, they dragged up an amount of brush, piled it into the opening, finally weighing it down with what rocks they could find.

Finished at last, they stood for a time looking at the lonely grave.

"Joe was a good old boy," Henry said. "Reckon I'll sure be

missing him."

The *vaquero* crossed himself, lowered his head. "Go to God, *viejo,*" he murmured. "I, too, will miss you."

Henry glanced at the pistol he had removed from Ely's rigid fingers. "Ain't taking this because I need it. Figure it's only right I get me a couple of them owlhoots with it . . . for old Joe's sake . . . when we catch up with them."

Dave stared off into the north. "If we catch up," he said heavily. "Come on, let's go."

X

It was late afternoon when they reached Eric Darrow's E-Bar-D Ranch. A hitched wagon stood in the driveway alongside the main house and several persons were moving about in the shade nearby.

Thirsty, hungry, bone-weary, the three men stumbled into the yard, halted first at the horse trough pump where they eased their burning throats and dashed water over their heads.

Ruskin, every muscle in his body aching from the long hike, the pain from the blow to the head still with him, finished first, turned to face Darrow and two of his hired hands as they moved up.

The rancher gave Dave and the men with him a sweeping glance. "What's all this about?"

There was no friendliness or concern in the man, only suspicion and hostility. Ruskin brushed at the water trapped in the bristles of his beard.

"We were driving a herd to Dalhart. Rustlers hit us. Got our horses along with every steer we had."

Darrow's expression altered slightly. "Where?"

"Red Bluff Crossing," Link Henry said, stepping up beside Dave. "Killed Joe Ely, winged Tibo. Would've nailed us, too, 'cepting we hid."

The rancher remained silent. At that moment the side door of the house opened and two women stepped out. One, graying and with a plain face, was apparently Eric Darrow's wife. The other was the girl Dave had seen in the buggy that morning in town when the ranchers had accosted him. Darrow's daughter, he guessed.

"Any idea who they were?"

At the rancher's question, Ruskin shook his head. "They wore masks. No brand on their horses . . . and it was dark."

Darrow shrugged. "Too bad about Joe Ely." He shifted his glance to Alveron, lounging against the trough, rolling a cigarette. "You need fixing up? My wife. . . ."

"Is nothing, *señor, gracias,*" the *vaquero* said before Darrow could finish.

"Could sure use a bite to eat," Link Henry commented hopefully.

Immediately Mrs. Darrow spun, reëntered the house. The girl came off the landing, crossed to stand beside her father.

"Main thing we need," Dave said, "is the loan of some horses. Like to get started hunting my herd soon as possible."

"Expect you would," the rancher said dryly. "You're getting a taste of what the rest of us have been putting up with for years."

Impatience shook Ruskin. "One thing . . . it ought to prove my uncle had nothing to do with the rustling you claim has been going on."

"Can't see as it does. Likely that bunch of hardcases Saul had hanging around are the ones behind this same as. . . ."

"It's got nothing to do with me," Dave snapped. "My place now, and those were my steers."

"Fact is," Link Henry said, "Jess Veetch and his bunch ain't. . . ."

"Never mind," Ruskin cut in angrily. "What about horses?"

The rancher shrugged. "Never yet turned away a man in

trouble, friend or not. Sending this wagon into town for some supplies. You can ride on it."

"Going back to town will cost me too much time. I need to get after the rustlers now."

"Afraid there's nothing I can do about that," Darrow said disinterestedly.

"There's plenty you can do! It's to your interest, and everybody else's, that I track down those thieves." Dave paused, brushed at the sweat accumulating on his face. "Let me have a horse for myself. Link and Tibo can go on into town. I'll take it as a big favor."

"Favor," the rancher echoed, eyes sparking. "Recollect asking Saul Gans for a favor once. You know what he done? Turned around, walked off. I'm doing the same."

"It's a little different now. I'm not Saul Gans."

"Far as I'm concerned, it's all the same."

"No, it isn't, Papa," the rancher's daughter said, shaking her head. "Not the same at all."

Darrow stiffened. "Now, Abby, keep out of this."

The girl turned to Dave. "I've a horse you can borrow. He's around back."

Ruskin's eyes met those of Abby Darrow. "I'm obliged, but I don't want to cause trouble."

"No trouble," she said lightly.

The rancher's voice was hard. "I won't have you going against me, Abby."

"Not that, Papa. It's just that I don't agree with you . . . and I always remember you said I should stand up for what I thought was right."

Darrow, face crimson, started to reply, hushed when his wife came through the doorway carrying a platter heaped with food.

"Bring the coffee, Abby," she said to the girl. "We'll serve them out on the back porch. Cooler there." Smiling at Dave and the others, she added: "This way."

Abby disappeared into the house. Darrow stepped back, and Dave, trailed by Link and Alveron, followed the rancher's wife to the verandah at the rear of the building where she set the tray on a table.

Pointing to the chairs, she said: "Make yourself comfortable. Expect you're tired. Abby'll be here with coffee in a minute." She turned away.

Link, taking up two slices of bread and a thick chunk of meat, fixed his eyes on Dave and leaned forward. "What's the sense in not telling Darrow about Veetch?"

Ruskin's jaw was set at a stubborn angle. "And have him and all the rest around here thinking they forced me to get rid of that bunch? I'm not about to give them the satisfaction."

"Ain't no time to be picky and mule-headed. Maybe, was I to explain to Eric. . . ."

"No. They'll hear about it soon enough. You won't be needing horses, anyway."

"You search for the herd alone?" Alveron asked.

Dave nodded. "It'll be better that way . . . faster," he said, and fell silent as Abby appeared with cups and a pot of coffee.

She placed them on the table without comment and walked off into the yard, apparently going after her mount.

"What do you want us to do?" Henry asked.

"Get back to the ranch . . . stay there. I'm worried now about the rest of the stock."

The old cowpuncher hesitated, stared. "You aiming to jump that bunch alone if you find them?"

Alveron's dark face sobered. "There were many. Twelve, fifteen. One man alone would have no chance."

"All I want to do is locate them. Then I'll get help."

"Help like Darrow's offering?" Link said dryly.

"They won't all feel the way he does . . . especially when I tell them I've got the rustlers spotted."

Link grunted. "You've got more faith in some folks than I have."

Ruskin grinned wryly. "Comes right back to the same old story . . . I haven't got much choice." Tipping his cup to his mouth, he downed the last of his coffee, rose to his feet. "Best I get started. Be dark in a couple of hours."

Link Henry, still eating, looked up. "Tibo and me can get horses in town. Might be smart, us cutting back, meeting you at the crossing. I sure don't like the idea you heading out alone."

"It's more important you get back to the ranch and keep watch over what stock I've got left. We lose them, I'm out of business for sure." Pivoting on a heel, he stepped off the porch. "So long."

Henry mumbled something. Alveron said—*"Muy bueno suerte."*—in a low, quiet tone.

Ruskin reached the end of the house, slanted to where Abby Darrow stood at a hitch rack, waiting for him at the head of a husky little buckskin. She smiled, handed him the reins.

"I expect the stirrups will need lengthening. I didn't have the time."

"They'll do," he said. "I don't like the idea of your crossing your father."

"Won't be the first time . . . and it'll blow over. Always has. Hope you find your herd."

Dave nodded, swung onto the saddle. "I'm obliged to you for the loan of your horse. I'll bring him back soon as I can."

"No hurry. I only wish I had two more so Link and the *vaquero* could go with you." She flicked a glance toward the house. "Several horses in the corral behind the barn. If you want to borrow them while nobody's looking. . . ."

Ruskin grinned. "And have your pa tacking horse thief signs on us? Don't think I want to take the chance." He glanced to the sun. "Thank your mother for me."

She nodded, stepped away. "Good luck."

Touching the brim of his hat, Dave nodded and rode out of the yard.

XI

As Dave Ruskin rounded the house, he glanced to the driveway. Alveron and Link Henry were climbing into the wagon, both crowding onto the seat beside the hired hand delegated to do the driving chore. Eric Darrow stood on the landing outside the kitchen door. He did not look up as Dave moved by.

Ruskin regretted the rancher's attitude. Darrow was being hard-nosed about everything, even to the point of heaping the hatred he had for Saul Gans upon Dave's head. Abby was something else. He'd seen disapproval for the ranchers in her eyes that morning in town, and she had displayed it again—along with a will of her own—by offering him her horse against the wish of her father.

Now, he wasted no time following the meandering course of Mestizo Creek. They had already done that *en route* to Darrow's, had found no place where the cattle had been driven out of the creekbed onto firm ground. Thus it was logical to assume the rustlers had headed south. Dave swore softly. If that morning they'd only decided to hike to Trigg's instead of to Darrow's—but they had chosen to go in the opposite direction. Unwittingly they had given the outlaws even a greater lead. He was confident, though, that on this horse, a good loper that took the hills and gullies with complete ease, he'd soon overcome the rustlers' advantage.

It was near dark when he reached the crossing at the bluffs. He paused there only long enough to breathe the buckskin, allow him to slake his thirst, and then pushed on. He chose a course directly down the center of the stream, holding the horse to a fast walk while his glance swung back and forth as he searched the banks for a break and telltale tracks.

The light faded gradually and it soon became difficult to see clearly. Finally he was forced to give up, fearing that he could possibly by-pass the sign he searched for. There was no more he could do until daylight, and, moving to a small coulée not far from the stream, he halted. Picketing the buckskin on the grass, he settled down to wait out the night.

He was on the move at first light, again in the channel through which the stream flowed, where he resumed his ceaseless probe of the steep banks. Eventually they would have to pull out; all he need do was find that point, and then he could begin tracking.

The slow search continued, and, as noon came, Ruskin was aware the stream had changed course, was veering sharply to the east. Abruptly he halted. The creek widened. The high banks began to melt away, finally disappearing into a larger stream crossing at right angles. The Tinaja, its east fork, he realized. Spurring forward eagerly, he studied the slope leading down on the opposite side to the wider creek. The soft, damp loam was unmarred, revealing no hoof prints.

Ruskin settled back wearily. The rustlers had evidently swung the cattle into the Tinaja, only a little deeper than Mestizo Creek, and were continuing on south. The problem of how the rustlers could keep the herd moving for so long a time in the creek became more of a puzzle. Cattle wouldn't bed down and rest in water—just as they balked at moving during the night hours. Then how . . . ?

Dave pulled up short, his glance on a half dozen steers standing in the shallows ahead of him. Drawing his pistol, he swung up onto dry land, cut around in a circle to where he was behind the animals. As he moved in close, his eyes picked up the brand on the nearest steer. Disappointment again slogged through him. Circle 8. He was on Floyd Trigg's range.

Abruptly he wheeled about, rode out of the brush onto higher ground. A fair-size herd of Trigg's cattle was grazing in a hollow below him. Needing to be convinced fully, he spurred into the scatter of cattle, checked closely. All carried Trigg's mark.

He couldn't understand it. Where could the outlaws have pulled out of the creekbed? Could he have missed the place—one that had been carefully brushed over by the rustlers to throw him off pursuit perhaps? That had to be it, he decided, angered at himself.

The sun's full blast now lay upon the land and a shimmering haze hung above the plains, distorting all that lay within eye's reach. He'd lost the rustlers for sure. There was only one thing left—go to Dalhart, wait and hope the outlaws would bring the herd to that point in search of a buyer. If that failed, he was finished. His high-flung hopes and dreams were over—almost before they had begun.

He touched the buckskin with his spurs. Then the dull *thud* of hoof beats reached him, halted him again. Looking ahead, he saw three riders pulling out of the creek bottom. Two were familiar—Jess Veetch and Cully Moss. The third man he did not recognize. The trio halted abruptly when they saw him, then came forward slowly.

"Little off your range, ain't you?" Veetch asked coldly, pulling up. His face was set to hard lines.

Moss and the third man, astride a Circle 8 horse, spread out quietly, forming a crescent with Dave in the center.

"Looking for my herd," Ruskin said. A tenseness gripped him. He could expect nothing but trouble from Veetch and Moss, and they were in a position to do their worst.

"On Trigg's land?"

"Didn't know I was on his range. Rustlers drove my stock

into the creek. I've been following it." Dave paused, staring at Veetch. "Know anything about it?"

"What makes you think I would?" There was a sly smile on the man's lips when he replied, one that bordered on satisfaction, even triumph.

"Just asking."

Veetch settled back on his saddle. "Well, you're asking the wrong man . . . and you're 'way out of your territory. Best you move on. Ain't healthy around here for you."

"And it is for you, that it?"

"I come and go where I take a notion," Veetch said.

Ruskin swung about, found Moss blocking his path. A gust of anger swept him. "Something on your mind?"

Cully was unmoving for several moments. Finally he shrugged. "No, reckon not," he said, and, turning away, pulled aside.

Dave, pressure easing, and somewhat surprised, rode on. He had anticipated violence, a move on the part of the two men to get even; strangely they had passed up their opportunity. He found it hard to understand, but he wasted no time thinking about it.

He re-crossed the Tinaja, and headed back to Darrow's ranch, to explain that he was striking out for Dalhart, and would need Abby's horse for a few more days.

As he rode, he noticed the profusion of hoof marks left by Trigg's cattle. If the rustlers were smart, they would have driven the herd out of the creekbed close to Trigg's cattle. By wiping out the prints where the steers left the creek, there would be no way of telling where the exit had been made. Mingled with hoof marks left by Trigg's cattle, the rustlers would be able easily to drive the herd across the upper end of Circle 8 range and leave no trail. Abandoning any further search along the creek, he put the buckskin to a lope for Darrow's.

It was late in the afternoon when he reached the gate and turned into the yard. Remembering the hitch rack where the buckskin had been waiting, he cut across the front of the house, angled for that point.

He heard a door slam somewhere, and then Abby appeared suddenly, running toward him. Frowning, he pulled to a halt, came off the saddle.

"No . . . no!" the girl cried, waving him back. "Keep going . . . don't stop!"

Dave stared at her. "Why . . . ?"

"You've got to hurry . . . get away from here, Dave!" she said, throwing a glance over her shoulder. "They're hunting for you!"

"What for? Who?"

"The marshal. They think you killed Rufe Hyatt . . . near the crossing."

Ruskin's jaw sagged. "Me? I haven't laid eyes on him since that morning. . . ."

"I know. I was sure you didn't do it. But you'll have to run, hide until they. . . ."

"He ain't going nowhere!" Eric Darrow's voice came from the front of the house. "Raise your hands, Ruskin. Do it slow . . . careful."

XII

"You're loco, Darrow," Dave snapped. "I never shot Hyatt. Haven't seen him."

"Lying won't help none. Get his gun, Tuck. Come around from behind."

Dave watched the man with the rifle circle cautiously, a moment later felt a lightening at his hip when his pistol was lifted from the holster. He glanced at Abby. She pulled back a step or two, and was staring at him helplessly.

"Get him a fresh horse," the rancher said. "I'm taking him to Harvey Drace. Maybe hanging their boss'll put the fear of God into that wild bunch."

Ruskin smiled bleakly. "Lynched . . . not hung. Seems I'm convicted before I even get a trial."

"You'll get a trial, all right, but we'll just be going through the motions. Evidence we've got makes it a cinch."

"Evidence? What evidence?"

"Something you didn't figure on, that's for sure," Darrow said with satisfaction. "Your name, that's what. Rufe scratched it, or most of it, in the sand before he died. Pegged you for the killer."

Surprise again rocked Dave. He shook his head. "Some kind of a mistake. Wasn't me."

"Sure . . . was somebody else. Hyatt wrote your name down just for cussedness."

"Don't know why he did it, but I didn't kill him." Ruskin's mind was working frantically, struggling to understand all that was happening, striving to make sense of the words he was hearing.

"Where'd they find Hyatt?"

Darrow laughed. "Still trying to play it cozy, eh? Right where you left him . . . at the crossing."

"He wasn't there when I was. Alveron and Link Henry will tell you that."

"They were there this morning?"

"No. Was the day. . . ."

"But you were."

Dave nodded slowly. "Did pass close by, looking for my herd. But I never. . . ."

"That's when Rufe was ambushed. Last night or early this morning. You were the only one around . . . and he named you as his killer."

"Wasn't me," Ruskin said doggedly. "Sure, I rode by the crossing, but I didn't stop. Figured my herd would be somewhere farther south." He paused, then: "Makes no sense, anyway. Why would I murder Hyatt? Hardly knew him."

"How the hell would I know?" Darrow snarled. "Probably was over that proof he mentioned he was going to hand to the marshal."

"Proof?" Dave recalled vaguely that Link Henry had spoken of such.

"About what's been going on out at the Gans place, maybe tying in the rustling we've been having. Not important now, anyway. Rufe's dead and you killed him. Plain fact, no matter why you did it."

"It's a frame-up," Ruskin said wearily.

"You think anybody'll believe that?"

"I do," Abby Darrow said suddenly. "There's no reason for him to do it."

"No reason!" the rancher snorted. "Every reason in the world! He figured Rufe had something that would break up his little set-up at Gans's."

"He just got here!" Abby exclaimed. "How could he have anything to do with it . . . and there's no real proof that there was anything going on there in the first place!"

"Don't prove a thing. We've got Ruskin dead to rights. Hyatt fixed that for us."

"If he did the writing."

"What's that?" Darrow demanded. "Who else would've? Was nobody else around except Ruskin."

"Somebody was," Dave said quietly.

The rancher's brows pulled to a straight line. "Who?"

"The man who found Hyatt's body."

"Oh, him. Was one of Floyd Trigg's riders. Jake something-

or-other. Seen Rufe's horse, cut over, found the body. Then got the marshal."

"What makes you think he couldn't have murdered Hyatt?"

"Jake? Now why the hell would he . . . ?"

"If you're going to lay it on anybody that was at the crossing, then he's as much a suspect as me."

"Only Rufe didn't write Jake's name. He wrote yours," Darrow said smugly. He looked up. Tuck was approaching, leading three saddled horses. "Where you been? Sure took you long enough."

The old cowpuncher shrugged, halted.

Darrow said: "Now get some cord, tie his hands behind him."

Tuck wheeled again, trotted toward the barn. Dave studied the rancher, tried to estimate his chance for escape. The other hired hand who had appeared with Tuck was standing a little to one side, not far from Abby. Darrow himself, pistol never lowering, was in front of the horses. The only protective cover of consequence, a shed, was a considerable distance away. He'd never reach it. Darrow would cut him down before he could cover a half dozen steps. But he had to do something. Once locked in Harvey Drace's jail, it would be all over for him. He'd never be able to convince an Apache Wells jury that he was innocent—not with the kind of evidence they had against him.

Tuck returned almost immediately. Moving to the rear of Ruskin, he pulled the tall man's hands together roughly, lashed his wrists securely. Without waiting for orders from Darrow, he pushed Dave toward the nearest horse, boosted him onto the saddle.

"Reckon he's ready," Tuck said.

"All right, let's move out," Darrow said as he swung onto his own mount. "I'll lead, you follow . . . keep him between us. Ain't letting him get away."

Abby Darrow, lips set, stepped up and halted beside Ruskin.

"Anything I can do . . . to help?"

Dave shrugged. "Be obliged if you'll get word to Link Henry. Tell him and the others to stick close to the ranch, look after things. I'll work this thing out somehow."

The girl nodded. "I'll go first thing."

"You'll do no such thing!" Darrow said sternly, leaning toward his daughter. "You'll stay here where you won't get in any trouble. I won't have you mixing in this. All hell's likely to break loose when news gets around that we've nailed Ruskin."

Abby faced her father soberly. "I'll do what I think's right," she said in a low voice, and then smiled at Dave. "Don't worry. I believe you . . . and there'll be others, too."

Ruskin managed a faint grin. "Good to know somebody's on my side," he said.

XIII

It was a hot, painful ride to Apache Wells for Dave Ruskin. With his hands lashed behind him, he was pinned to the saddle in an unnatural position, and almost at once his shoulders began to ache. As they entered town, every muscle in his body was screaming.

They turned into the main street at sundown. Several persons were on the boardwalks, a few in stores, and, as the small column began its passage down the dusty way to the marshal's office, word spread quickly, a hot flame in dry brush. A noisy crowd began to collect and follow.

Ruskin saw Tuck glance nervously over his shoulder, heard him say: "Better move right along, Mister Darrow. Them folks act real ugly."

"They've got a right," the rancher replied. "Rufe was thought a lot of around here. Don't reckon it'd make much difference if they just sort of took over. Save holding a trial."

Dave listened in grim silence. Darrow would as soon turn

him over to a lynching party as draw his next breath. And then he sighed in quiet relief. Up ahead Henry Drace, a shotgun cradled in his arms, had emerged from his quarters and was moving forward to meet them.

The lawman, face hard, moustache bristling, halted in the center of the street. He allowed Darrow, Ruskin, and Tuck to pass, and then took up a stand directly behind them, blocking the oncoming crowd.

"Ain't nothing any of you are looking for down this way," he said in a flat voice. "Just go on back, get about your business."

A chorus of yells went up. Drace allowed the shotgun to swing about, almost carelessly, but ready for use.

"Hate to see any of you folks get hurt, but that's what's going to happen if you don't do like I say."

The gathering remained motionless for several moments, and then two or three members turned, moved back to the walk. Others began to drift away, still muttering among themselves but reluctant to test the lawman's will.

Drace did not stir until the last had gone, and then, wheeling, retraced his steps to the front of the jail where Dave and the others were yet on their saddles.

"Get him inside . . . out of sight," the marshal directed. "Once he's locked up they'll settle down."

Darrow swung stiffly from his horse. "Be a good thing if they did grab him."

"They won't," Drace snapped. "And I want no more talk like that from you, Eric . . . or anybody else."

Standing at the side of the open doorway, he pushed Ruskin into the jail's single cell, removed his gun belt, and slashed the cord that bound his wrists. Backing out, he slammed the grating, locked it.

"Where'd you find him?"

"My place," Darrow said. "Come riding in, big as you please."

The lawman frowned. "Plenty of gall," he said, and tossed the ring of keys onto his desk.

"Was returning a horse . . . borrowed it from Abby," Dave said. "No reason why I'd be afraid to go there."

Darrow ignored him and turned to Drace. "Figured you'd be out with a posse."

"Have been. Just rode in an hour or so ago. Aimed to head out again after dark. He admit to killing Rufe?"

Darrow shrugged. "No, claims he. . . ."

"I can do my own talking," Dave broke in angrily. "The answer's no, Marshal. I didn't. Haven't laid eyes on Hyatt since that morning here in town."

Drace leaned against a corner of his desk. "Yeah, and I'm remembering what you said to him . . . all them threats. Pretty strong evidence we've got against you. We know you were at the crossing . . . and that name Rufe wrote before he died."

"He was wrong."

"Could be," the lawman said. "Could've got only a glimpse of the man who jumped him and thought it was Ruskin."

The rancher's face darkened. "Who the hell's side you on, Harvey?"

"Nobody's," Drace replied coolly. "But I aim to look at it from all sides, get at the truth."

"Leave that to the jury," Darrow said. "They'll do the deciding."

"After I've told them all there is to know about it." The marshal turned his attention to Dave. "There anybody you want to talk to?"

Ruskin shook his head. Abby Darrow would get word to Link and the others at the ranch, not that they could be expected to help any. As far as the town was concerned, he could think of no one who could even remotely be considered a friend.

Drace looked at the clock on the wall. "Tobin ought to be

getting here. Soon as he does, we'll go get a bite to eat at my place."

"Don't want to be no bother," Darrow said. "Me and Tuck can go to the restaurant."

"Won't hear of it . . . here's Tobin now."

Dave watched a lean, middle-aged man wearing a star step into the doorway, pause, his eyes on the cell.

"Hear you got him," he said.

"I did," Darrow said, smiling.

Harvey Drace turned for the exit. "Keep an eye on the street," he said. "Don't figure there'll be any trouble unless that bunch around Fred Banner's gets liquored up enough to start feeling brave."

Tobin nodded, moved the lawman's chair, and sat down. "Ain't likely."

"Something does start, shoot off that shotgun. I'll come quick."

Again the deputy bobbed his head. Ruskin watched the three men step into the open. The jail was silent, stuffy with trapped heat and faint sounds coming from the street, echoing in a muted, hollow way.

Tobin rose suddenly, crossed to a corner of the room, and dipped himself a drink of water from the bucket standing on a small table. Finished, he looked at Dave.

"Want one?"

"Be obliged to you," Ruskin said.

The older man filled the tin dipper again, approached cautiously, holding the ladle at arm's length. Dave grinned, shook his head, and accepted the container. He downed the drink, then returned the dipper.

"This Jake, man who found Hyatt's body . . . you know him?"

"Some," Tobin said, settling into Drace's chair once more.

"For long?"

"Ain't been around but three, maybe four months."

"Mostly a stranger."

"Reckon so. Why?"

"Trying to get things straight in my head. Wasn't me that killed Hyatt, and if this Jake is the only other man who saw him. . . ."

Tobin lifted a broad hand for silence, came to his feet, face turned to the door. A low muttering of voices was arising in the street. Immediately the deputy crossed to the opening, glanced out. He remained there for only moments, then slammed the door and bolted it. Recrossing the room, he snatched up the shotgun, sank down on a corner of Drace's desk.

"Reckon we're having company after all."

XIV

Dave stared at the deputy. "Better do what the marshal said . . . fire off that gun . . . warn him."

Tobin stirred. "Ain't no hurry. Could be they're just horsin' around."

"No time for guessing. It's my neck at stake."

"Don't worry none about it. I can handle them."

The racket in the street had increased, and was now a sullen threat directly in front of the jail. Dave gripped the bars of his cell, rattled them violently.

"Damn it, man . . . either signal the marshal or give me a gun! I've got a right to protect myself."

The deputy shook his head. "They find that door locked, they'll back off, forget. . . ."

His words were lost in the splintering sound the panel made as it gave way under booted feet. A thick-bodied man, eyes inflamed by too much liquor, and closely followed by a half dozen others, crowded in. Behind them a small crowd piled up on the landing, shouting and shoving.

"Turn him loose, Deputy," the squat man ordered. "We got things all ready for him."

Tobin appeared stunned, unable to believe what had happened. Abruptly he recovered. Stepping back against the wall quickly, he leveled the shotgun at the tightly knotted group.

"Get out of here, Gabe. You ain't taking no prisoner away from me."

Gabe grinned. The men standing behind him began to fan out slowly. One suddenly bent forward, snatched the ring of keys from the top of the lawman's desk. Tobin whirled angrily to him. In that same moment Gabe lunged, caught the barrel of the weapon in his hands, wrenched it from the deputy's grasp.

"Reckon that takes care of that," he said, grinning widely. Turning his head to the street, he shouted: "We got him!"

Ruskin, face grim, stood in the center of his cell and waited. He watched Gabe stand the shotgun against the wall, motion to the man with the keys.

"Open it up, Earl."

Tobin made a futile attempt to stop the man, but sank back as two others caught him by the shoulders.

"You just stay quiet, Deputy," one said. "Ain't no sense you getting hurt."

"The marshal'll have you all in jail for this!" Tobin shouted, struggling weakly. "I'll give him names, every one of you. . . ."

"Sure you will . . . and you'll be doing your duty, just like you ought. Marshal can't expect no more'n that."

The man called Earl fitted the key into the lock. Dave heard the sharp *click* as the tumblers released. The grating swung open.

"All right, bushwhacker," Gabe said, beckoning with a thick forefinger. "Come on out."

Ruskin stared at him, mind working swiftly. The shotgun was to his right, only a stride away. He lowered his head resignedly.

"You're lynching the wrong man," he said in a quiet voice.

Gabe laughed loudly. "Sure, sure. Ain't nobody ever guilty of nothing. Come on, less'n you want me dragging you out."

Ruskin started forward, head still bowed. He passed through the cell's opening. Gabe and the man next to him reached out. Instantly Dave hurled himself at the pair. His shoulder drove into Gabe's bulk; his elbow caught the second man in the throat. As the pair slammed back into the men behind them, Ruskin whirled. With a sweep of his arm he grabbed up the shotgun, leveled it at the startled crowd.

"Get him!" Gabe yelled.

Dave swung the stock of the weapon in a short, vicious circle. There was a sharp, cracking sound as it struck Gabe just above the ear. The thick-set man dropped solidly.

"Start backing for the door," Ruskin ordered tautly. "You, too," he added, jerking his head at Tobin.

All but the senseless Gabe began to shift toward the opening.

"Anybody tries using a gun on me, you in the front will get both barrels," he warned. "Tell them!"

Earl, fear pulling his features into sagging lines, glanced anxiously to the street. "You . . . out there! Don't do nothing! He's covering us with a scatter-gun!"

Following closely, Dave backed the crowd into the open, motioned them to one side with the barrels of his weapon. "This gun'll be on you all the time," he said in a slow, promising way. "Don't get any ideas unless you want a charge of buckshot in the belly."

Slowly he began to retreat toward the corner of the building. There'd be an alley behind it and the row of buildings adjacent. If he could reach it, he'd have a chance.

"You won't get far!" Tobin shouted, taking a short step. Dave moved the shotgun slightly. "You won't be going anywhere if you make a move like that again."

The deputy froze.

Ruskin continued slowly, then reached the corner. "Stay put," he warned softly, and moved hurriedly along the side of the building. Gaining the alley with its deep shadows, he stopped, keeping the twin muzzles of the shotgun in view. The crowd could not see him clearly, he knew, only the barrels of the weapon. But the instant they were certain he had gone, they'd come surging after him. If he could delay them for only a few moments. . . . He glanced about. His eyes fell upon an empty crate an arm's length away.

Keeping the shotgun pointed at the crowd, he dragged the crate to the corner of the building. Then, moving carefully, he laid the weapon across its top, exposing only the muzzles. From the street it would appear that he was still there—an assumption that would hold long enough, he hoped, to permit his finding a safe hiding place.

Pivoting, he trotted silently off into the alley, eyes sweeping back and forth in search of a suitable hiding place. He wouldn't need to hang around for long—an hour, two at the most—but during that time he could expect a thorough search for him to be under way, headed undoubtedly by Harvey Drace.

The gaunt bulk of a deserted stable loomed up on his right. The doors and windows were open, some missing entirely, but the slightly pitched roof with its high false front offered possibilities.

Shouts back near the jail warned him that his trick had been discovered. The crowd would be coming now, swarming down the alley, probing along the buildings. He ducked immediately into the doorway of the weathered old barn.

For a few moments he stood in the murky gloom, and then his eyes located the ladder leading up to the loft. He crossed the width of the building to it, leaping over the accumulation of trash and discarded timbers that blocked the one-time runway.

Instantly he began to ascend and quickly gained the loft. He was well above the ground but he'd find no safety there for long.

Hurrying to the front, he peered out of the loft window. The street lay directly below. Men were rushing past, yelling to each other. There was no time to lose. Wheeling, he crossed to the rear of the building to where faint twilight filtered in from a hole in the roof. It was too small to permit his crawling through, but it was a means to the roof itself.

Placing his hands against the boards, he pushed hard. One gave readily. Working it aside, he grasped a joist, pulled himself up, and boosted himself through the opening. A sigh slipped from his lips as he paused to brush away the sweat clothing his forehead. He'd made it.

Hunching low, and careful to place his weight on a joist, he moved toward the tall, warped false front of the structure. Reaching it, he followed along its base until he found an opening where one of the neglected boards had pulled away from the studding, thus affording him a good view of the street.

He sprawled out full length. He should be safe. The angle of the roof would hide him from anyone thorough enough to climb up and look through the hole; the false front shielded him from those below. All he need do was to wait for the search to die off. He could then make good his escape.

XV

The day's heat soaked up by the weathered boards seeped through his clothing, brought sweat pouring from his body, but he did not move. Coolness would come soon and it would not be so bad.

The hunt was in full swing. Drace and Darrow had returned, and, after an angry conversation with Tobin and several others in front of the jail, things had gotten organized. The marshal had called everyone along the street to a hurried meeting. Then, breaking the volunteers into parties of three, a systematic search along the street, alleys, and passageways had begun. Orders evidently were to pass up no possibilities, take nothing for granted.

Dave grinned tightly. They'd check the old barn, too, probe not only the scattered débris on the ground floor but the loft as well. So far he had noticed no one on any roof. Such was being overlooked, he guessed—and hoped it would hold true.

Two riders entered town from the east. He recognized Veetch and Cully Moss. It had been one of Trigg's men he'd seen with them earlier that day, and he wondered idly if the pair had taken jobs with the big, red-haired rancher. Perhaps the whole crew had signed up with him. That would be a bit strange, he decided; Trigg had been one of the ranchers who'd complained loudly about them.

He watched the two men dismount at the hitch rack in front of Fred Banner's. They paused for a minute to look down the street, and then disappeared inside.

Darkness gradually spread over the settlement, showing first along the sidewalks, slowly creeping up the walls of the buildings and houses. Lamps came on in the stores, laying strips of mellow light upon the ankle-deep dust. The bell at the church began to toll, and somewhere a dog barked frantically.

"Kept going . . . I'll lay odds on it."

The voice, so unexpectedly near, startled Ruskin. He lay absolutely motionless, scarcely breathing. A moment later he realized the speaker was directly below him, standing in the entrance to the barn.

"Grabbed hisself a horse, lit out while we was still standing back there in front of the jail like a bunch of dummies."

"Would've heard a horse," a second voice protested.

"Not if he walked him to the edge of town, then mounted.

Marshal'd do better getting a posse together and taking out after him."

"Wouldn't know which way he went."

"Didn't head south, we know that. Leaves three other roads. Break the posse up into three bunches."

"About what Harvey'll be doing next. He's sure riled up over him getting away."

"You figure he done it . . . killed Rufe, I mean? Claims he didn't."

"Hell, you think he'd admit it? Not much! Was I to put a couple of bullets straight into a man's heart, you think I'd tell the law it was me that pulled the trigger?"

There was a pause. Then: "Must be right good shot . . . two bullets in the heart."

"Nothing good about it at all. Got Hyatt from behind, in the back. Was standing so close it set his shirt afire."

Deeply within Dave Ruskin's mind something stirred, began to clamor for recognition. He frowned, tried to concentrate. Abruptly his attention was caught by a dry, scraping sound beneath him. He tensed. A third man making a search of the loft. The hole in the roof . . . if he noticed that, decided to investigate. . . .

The noise ceased. A different, voice called out: "Ain't up here! Let's try next door!"

"He's gone. Kept right on running."

"Sure be a fool to be hanging around."

"Maybe so, but the marshal said we was to look everywhere, and, mad as he is, I sure ain't figuring to cross him."

One of the three swore. Silence followed. Dave remained quiet, the clamoring within him renewing itself. Suddenly it clarified in his mind. *Shot in the heart.* The rancher would have died instantly! He would have been totally unable to do anything, much less scratch a name in the sand.

Ruskin stirred angrily. What the hell was wrong with Harvey Drace? Couldn't he see that? It would prove the killer was someone else, that he had written the name in an effort to shift the blame. That someone was framing him for the murder was evident, just as he had suspected at the start. There was little comfort in the thought that he had been right, however; he'd never get the chance to point out the hole in the evidence Drace and the others were setting so much stock by.

Something else nagged at him—Veetch and Cully Moss. What were they doing on Circle 8 range? It didn't seem logical that Floyd Trigg would hire them, yet they spoke and acted as if they were on home ground, not just riding across the rancher's land. Suddenly he recalled exactly where he had encountered them—near the crossing. Had they seen Rufe Hyatt? Could it have been one of them who ambushed the rancher?

Dave wrestled with his thoughts, tried to puzzle out the questions, fit it all into some sort of pattern. But something didn't jibe. He shifted again to ease his throbbing muscles, looked down into the street. The search was slackening. A half dozen men were standing in front of the jail. Back in the direction of Banner's three more were returning slowly, heading for the same point.

He rolled over, glanced at the sky. Full dark had come and stars were beginning to make themselves visible. The moon, a faint crescent of silver, was almost lost in a bank of stringy clouds.

He should be able to leave his hide-out soon. He'd wait until all the search parties had returned to Harvey Drace's office, then climb down, somehow manage a horse, and leave town.

Then what? Run—get out of the country? Forget the ranch in Fire Valley? The cards were all stacked against him; the odds were all wrong. Here he had only enemies, excepting his loyal ranch hands and Abby Darrow—all of whom deserved better than being dragged into a hopeless fight.

But it was not in Dave Ruskin to run. It was his land, his ranch, his cattle he was being compelled to fight for—along with his right to live. And there was no future in running, not with the label of killer tacked to his name. Better to settle it. Better to try and clear his name, settle once and for all time his claim to what was his—or go down fighting.

Pulling himself to a crouch, he began to work his way back to the hole in the roof. It was time to move out.

XVI

Ruskin dropped to the barn's loft quietly, made his way down the ladder, and reached the ground level. He could hear someone in the street in front of the old building, and pulled himself back into the shadows against the wall. A man and a woman walked hurriedly past the open doorway. Intent in conversation, they gave no attention to the interior of the abandoned structure.

Breath easing, Ruskin waited until they were out of sight and, then turning, crossed to the rear of the structure. Again halting, he made a quick but thorough inspection of the littered alley. He saw no one and quickly moved on.

The stable lay to his right, a low, sprawling affair almost at the end of the street. It would be necessary to pass the rear of four or five business houses *en route,* but all were dark and apparently closed.

Keeping close to the walls, he covered the distance hurriedly, halted finally at a maze of corrals behind the livery barn. A light burned in the small office in the front, and for a time he stood motionlessly in the darkness, studying that. He saw no silhouettes moving about, concluded no one was there, and continued on through the corrals, following out a passageway between the split poles until he came to the rear entrance of the building.

The muffled sound of hoof beats was coming from the street. He paused. Somewhere along the way a man sang out a greeting. Faint music drifted from Banner's, the strains interrupted now and then by a shout or laughing.

Ruskin took a long breath, stepped through the wide opening into the rank-smelling darkness of the barn, again stopped. He was at the end of a runway. At the opposite point, where the structure faced the street, a man, sitting in a chair tipped back against the door's frame, was snoring softly. Behind him a hanging lantern surrounded him with a small pool of yellow light.

Tense, taking each step with care for fear of stumbling over some unseen object, Dave crossed to the row of stalls, began to work forward. Luck favored him. In the third compartment he found the horse he had ridden in from Darrow's. The two other animals were in the adjacent stalls. All were still saddled and bridled, an indication that the rancher had intended to return home that night.

Laying his hand on the horse's rump and murmuring softly, Ruskin moved to the front of the box, groped about until he found the neck rope. Releasing the spring hook from the ring, he allowed it to drop into the manger. Then, praying the tall bay would not make too much noise, he backed the horse into the runway.

The stableman was not disturbed. When Dave glanced at him, his eyes were still closed. Stepping to the head of the bay, Ruskin led him through the rear exit, down the lane between the corrals, and once again reached the alley.

He swung onto the saddle immediately, wishing now he had taken time to check the scabbards on the other mounts for a rifle. He'd need a weapon—but it was too late now. He'd best try and get one elsewhere. Returning to the stable would be too risky.

Clucking to the bay, he headed off into the darkness, moving northward for the edge of town. The question was before him again: *What next?*

He had proof, more or less, that Rufe Hyatt had not been the one to scrawl his name in the sand, but such was of little real value at the moment. He needed more, needed actually to identify the murderer. But where does a man start to look for a phantom?

The recollection of Jess Veetch, his ever-present shadow, Cully Moss, and the rider from Trigg's Circle 8 came to mind, began once more to prod him relentlessly. Something about that disturbed him. Could it be that the suspicion with which local ranchers regarded the one-time foreman and crew of Saul Gans had foundation? Were they responsible for the cattle rustling that had taken place in the area? Was it possible that Veetch and his crowd were working with one, or perhaps several, of Floyd Trigg's men, operating a rustling ring under the rancher's unsuspecting nose? Trigg's place, being the farthest east and therefore not only beyond sight of other ranchers, but much nearer the cattle market and railhead as well, would be ideally situated for such activities.

His own herd had disappeared in that general locality; later he had encountered Veetch, Cully, and Trigg's man. Was there a connection? Further, Rufe Hyatt's body had been found not far distant. Was that more than a coincidence?

The Circle 8. Probably in some remote corner of Trigg's vast spread there'd be a hidden corral where stolen cattle could be driven unseen by others—even Floyd Trigg himself—and there the brands could be blotted for later sale of the stock in Dalhart. Perhaps it had been proof of such that had brought death to Rufe Hyatt, as Darrow had suggested. Fearing it, the rustlers had ambushed him, and then, in a display of exceptional forethought, left a clue designed to fix the blame upon a man already at odds with Fire Valley.

It all stood to reason, and, while there were gaping holes in the theory, there was also a great deal of logic and ordinary horse sense. Regardless, Dave realized it was all he had to go on. He could do nothing but pursue his reasoning, and hope he might remain free until he had uncovered the truth.

The bay stopped of its own accord. Ruskin, deep in thought, glanced up. They had reached the edge of the settlement.

" 'Evenin'," a voice said from the corner of the last building in the row fronting the street.

Dave lowered his face, tugged at his hat. "A fine one."

A shadow detached itself from the darkness, and took up a position at the end of the board sidewalk.

"Don't I know you?"

"Doubt it. Just riding through."

Ruskin urged the bay on, keeping him to a casual walk, fearing to show haste.

"Kind of funny," the man said. "That there's an E-Bar-D horse you're riding. Belongs to Eric Darrow. Mind telling me where you got him?"

Dave swore silently. He'd come so close, so near to a clean escape, but his voice was level when he replied.

"Borrowed him. Mine strayed. Darrow let me have this one till I could chase down. . . ."

"That's a god-damn lie!" the man in the dark shouted suddenly, grabbing for his pistol. "You're the jasper they're all hunting!"

Ruskin plunged home his spurs, swerved the startled bay straight at the man. The fellow yelled, dodged to one side. He tripped over the raised edge of the walk, went down, weapon blasting harmlessly into the night's calm.

Dave, bent low over the bay's arched neck, drove hard for the first outcropping of brush 100 yards distant. The pistol racketed again, and then a shout lifted.

"Marshal . . . here he is! Heading north! Marshal!"

XVII

Ruskin gained a slight rise, allowed the hard-breathing bay horse to slow, catch his wind. He looked back. Riders were streaming out of the town, dark silhouettes flashing across a scatter of lights at the end of the street. Harvey Drace had been shaping up his posse at the very moment the alarm was sounded. Again Dave swore. He'd not figured on a gun-happy searching party dogging his heels while he tried to work out his problems.

Moving off the hill, he found himself on the fringe of the broad flat known as the Apache Plains, and began to veer steadily west. His best hope for shaking the posse would lie in the rough country near Red Bluff Crossing, not on the open prairie where even in the pale starlight a rider could be seen for a considerable distance.

Once more he looked over his shoulder. Drace and his men were coming on in a tight bunch—and they were close. Somehow they'd gained on him. He doubled forward on the bay, pressed the big horse for more speed. He couldn't hope to keep up the headlong pace for any length of time, but if he could build up a decent lead, he should be able to maintain it. The posse horses, too, would begin to tire.

But one thing was certain now. The posse had killed his plan of looking over the country east of Trigg's ranch where he felt he might find his stolen cattle. He guessed now he'd be smart to head for Dalhart, endeavor to enlist the aid of the law there. He'd be running a risk, that was certain, but the sheriff of the railhead town would not be so close to the incidents that had occurred in Fire Valley; perhaps he'd readily see that Dave was being wrongly accused of murder.

The fact that he was riding in, presenting himself willingly, would further work in his favor. Dave grinned into the darkness. Maybe he was fooling himself, talking himself into a situation that could kick back, put him in real trouble. But he'd have to take that risk. His life wasn't worth a plugged copper where Harvey Drace and his posse members were concerned. His hanging was inevitable.

The bay began to lag. Ruskin glanced back. The posse was a vague blur in the soft silver of the night and a considerable distance away. He felt a stir of relief. The horse had more than held his own—and the steady grind had begun.

He tried to figure where he was. Still miles from the crossing, he supposed, but not too far from Trigg's. He'd best be careful, swing wide of the place. He didn't want to attract Circle 8 riders to the chase.

Time wore on to the steady *thud* of the bay's hoofs. Gradually the country began to break up, show more low hills, arroyos, and bluffs. He was drawing near the crossing, approaching from a different angle and some distance south of the point where the encounter with the rustlers had taken place. There was brush all along the stream, and once he'd reached that his chances for shaking the posse would be greatly improved.

He glanced around, felt a tremor of surprise. The number of pursuing horsemen had decreased. A moment later he saw groups of riders off to either side of the main party. Drace had split his men, was endeavoring to sweep around him from both sides, force him into a pocket.

Ruskin brushed at the sweat on his face wearily. He doubted he could outrun the encircling parties with the tired bay. He'd have to duck into the brush, seek safety in the deep shadows.

He reached the stream's channel, swung right along its bank

until he found a less abrupt point where he could drop down to the creek's level. Spurring the bay across the shallow water, he plunged into the undergrowth, continued south for 100 yards or so, and then, in a dense thicket of willow and dogwood, halted.

The bay was trembling, near exhaustion. Dave swung from the saddle, moved off a few paces to where he could hear above the horse's sucking for air. The rhythmic pounding of oncoming horses slightly west marked the position of Harvey Drace and the main body of riders. He could hear nothing of the groups above and below him.

The lawman had played it smart. He'd figured his fugitive would attempt to hide along the stream. He would now string one faction of his posse along the west side, direct them to work in from that point, thus trap their objective in between.

Ruskin continued to listen. He could hear voices, first in the area where Drace was, and then coming from below, and finally above as the parties began to converge. After a few moments he returned to the bay. The horse was standing quietly, head down. He had recovered his wind, but the best was gone from him.

Dave studied him briefly while he came to decision, and then, pausing momentarily to pat the animal's corded neck, he moved off into the shadows, pointing downstream. He covered no more than fifty steps when a man's cautious voice, coming from the bank above, brought him to abrupt stop.

"See anything?"

"Nothing . . . so far."

The reply was so near that Ruskin froze instantly, fearing even to turn.

"Probably got him running toward Harvey and the others. Sure ain't come up onto the flat yet."

"Maybe turned north."

Dave watched the speaker pass by, a small, wiry man, his face hidden under the wide brim of his hat. He'd encounter the worn bay shortly, Ruskin thought. It could afford him the opportunity he needed.

Only when the rustling of the man's passage had faded did Ruskin break his stance. The posse member was out of sight in the depths of the brush. Immediately Dave wheeled to the steep wall of the cut, and clawed his way to the top.

Flat on his belly, he crawled over the edge and out to where he could see. Two riders, leading a third horse, were just above him. They were walking their mounts slowly, keeping pace with the man below. Suddenly both halted. The bay had been discovered.

The two riders dismounted hurriedly. Ground-reining their horses, they moved to the edge of the cut, dropped over the side into the brush. Instantly Ruskin drew himself upright and, running lightly, sprinted to where the horses waited.

Reaching the first, the one being led, he snatched up the reins and quietly moved away, pulling directly back from the gully where he could hear a muttering of voices. Vaulting onto the saddle, he swung the horse about sharply and headed eastward. Harvey Drace hadn't trapped him yet.

XVIII

Ruskin figured he'd shaken Harvey Drace and the posse. No more had been heard from them after he slipped quietly off from the edge of the gully where the stream flowed. The rolling contour of the land made it impossible to tell if he were being followed. But if he couldn't see them because of the country's conformation, they would be unable to locate him.

He noticed a light—far to his right. It appeared to be a lamp shining through a window. The Trigg place, he assumed. It should lie in that direction. If so, he was far below the usual trail to the railhead.

Accordingly he began to angle north slightly, and found himself entering a rough, broken country of many arroyos, small cañons, and sandy washes. Creosote bush, rabbitweed, ironwood, and cholla cactus grew shoulder high, and the little black gelding he had appropriated from the posse member began to slow his pace as the going became increasingly difficult. Ruskin understood then why the cattle drives followed the route farther north, deliberately avoiding the brake in which cattle could become easily lost and travel would be time-consuming.

Suddenly Dave pulled the black to a stop. The faint flicker of a small fire well to his right in a deep wash had caught his eye. Raising himself in the stirrups, he tried to make out the camp, but it was too dark and the basin too distant to make definition possible. One of Trigg's cow camps? It didn't seem reasonable. He was on Circle 8 range, he knew, but the cattleman would hardly maintain a camp in that desolate, useless area.

Curious, he swung the black from the course he was following, pointed for the small red eye glowing in the darkness. It was just possible he had stumbled upon the very thing for which he had intended to search—the rustlers' hide-out.

Dave glanced at the rifle boot hanging from his saddle, and cursed softly. It was empty. He recalled, then, the man had been carrying his long gun as he probed the brush-filled bed of Mestizo Creek. He was still without a weapon.

But he pressed on, doubling back in a wide circle to prevent making his approach noticeable, and coming in on the sink where the camp lay from its lower end. Drawing near the rim, all but hidden by dense growth, he dismounted a few yards short, tied the black to a clump of greasewood, and worked his way to the edge.

He'd overshot the camp. The fire was a considerable distance to his left, but he could make out the figures of a half dozen men sprawled around it. Horses stood nearby. And then he heard a sound to his right, and swung his attention to that direction. He could see nothing because of a rise, and, keeping low, he moved to the lip of the sink, looked down into a deep gash in the land.

Cattle. Satisfaction flowed through him. He'd found the rustlers' camp. But before he sought help from the nearest rancher—Floyd Trigg—he'd best make certain.

For long minutes he studied the motionless blur of the herd bedded in the steep walled, box-like coulée, making sure there were no riders on watch, and then he slipped over the edge and made his way to the sleeping animals.

The first steer he examined bore the brand of Saul Gans—a single S. He saw more, and knew at once it was the herd he had lost. Then he began to encounter other marks—the E-Bar-D of Eric Darrow, the Tumbling A of Amos Pool, Hyatt's Double-D.

Ruskin grinned tightly. He'd hit the jackpot. Here were cattle belonging to every rancher in the area, all gathered and waiting to be driven to Dalhart or some different railhead for disposal. Here was the proof he needed, and nearby were the rustlers themselves.

He climbed back to the overlooking flat, pondered his best move. He had no weapon, and against a half dozen ruthless outlaws he couldn't hope to win. In fact, attempting to do something on his own could result in the rustlers' escaping.

Best follow his initial inclination, to get help from Trigg. He knew definitely where the ranch lay, while the location of the posse was impossible to guess. Trigg's was not far, if the light he had seen was at the Circle 8 ranch house, and he was fairly certain of that. He smiled, thinking of the red-headed rancher's reaction when told the rustlers were maintaining their camp almost in the shadow of his own buildings. He'd get a lot of satisfaction making Trigg and the others—Darrow, Harvey Drace, and Pool—eat their words.

It was smart to play it safe, however. He'd get a look at the rustlers, see who they were. Then, if something occurred in the meantime and they fled before he could return with help, he'd know for whom to look.

Dropping back to the black, and keeping well away from the rim of the sink, he led the horse to a point just below the faint glare of the fire. Again securing him, he dropped low, crawled to the rim.

There were seven men directly opposite. All appeared to be sleeping except two. Hunched near the flickering flames, they had a bottle that they were passing back and forth. Ruskin strained to make out their identities in the poor light.

Anger stirred him, but strangely he was not greatly surprised. Both had been hired hands of Saul Gans—Gries and Baker. Likely the others had been in the crew, also—and all were followers of Jess Veetch. The ranchers had been right about them.

"Where you heading when we're done with this bunch?" It was Tom Gries who had spoken. Fresh anger shot through Ruskin. If only he had a gun!

"South," Baker said. "Maybe across the border. Got myself a pretty good little stake now."

Gries took a long pull at the bottle. "Wish't I could say the same. Me, I'm flat busted. All I'll have is what I've got coming."

"Won't be much. Ain't no more'n a couple hundred head."

"Be something . . . and a damn' sight better than nothing. When we moving out?"

"Couple of days," Baker said.

"Hope so. Getting mighty tired laying out here in the sticks. Sure hard on a man's bones."

"One more night ought to be the last of it."

"We doing the branding tomorrow?"

"Reckon so. Boss said he'd send Jess down with the irons first thing in the morning."

XIX

Dave Ruskin stiffened with surprise. The words of the outlaw stuck in his mind. The boss! Who was the boss? He had simply assumed Jess Veetch to be the leader of the rustlers; it appeared now that he was no more than one of the hirelings.

A thought captured him, grew steadily into strong suspicion. It was an improbable idea—but it could be true. Taking pains to make no noise, he withdrew to his horse, mounted. He'd have to move fast. A faint lightening in the east warned him sunrise was not too far off and soon he'd lose the protection of darkness.

He pointed the black directly for Trigg's Circle 8, cutting across the brake to the high plain, and then, following a low ridge, came in to it from the north. The house and the crew's quarters still lay in shadowy silence when he pulled up to a lower corral and halted, but lamplight shone in the kitchen window, evidence that the cook was up and about.

Moving along the corral, Dave reached the barn, turned the corner, and crossed swiftly to the open doorway of the structure. Inside he paused.

Irons—branding irons—they were what he must find. He could be all wrong, he realized—looking in the wrong place, suspecting the wrong man. Baker had referred to someone he called the boss. It could be a man not even in Fire Valley, one living in Dalhart, perhaps. He shook his head at the thought.

"I'm right . . . I'm sure of it," he muttered grimly. Moving deeper into the barn, he began a methodic search for Trigg's branding irons. If what he suspected was true, there'd be several.

But after looking in all the likely places, he found none, which in itself was strange: a rancher ordinarily kept his markers hanging on a wall where they would be readily available. He returned to the doorway. Lamplight showed now in the bunkhouse. The crew was rousing. He didn't have much time left.

His glance came to a stop on a small open-fronted building a few paces to his left. Within it he could see a forge, several wagon wheels, other odds and ends, the blacksmith shop. Wheeling, he started for it.

Immediately a large dog that had apparently been sleeping near the rear of the main house leaped to his feet and began to bark. Dave swore, hurried on. The dog, yapping furiously, trotted into the center of the yard. Ruskin reached the smithy, ducked quickly inside.

At that moment the door of the crew's quarters was flung open and a voice shouted at the dog. The animal hushed and, growling sullenly, slinked back to his bed.

Dave, drawing an easier breath, waited until the dog had settled down, turned then to the shed at the back of the shop. Immediately his eyes picked up the line of irons hanging on the wall. He crossed hastily, made a complete examination. All were Circle 8.

Disappointed, he halted in the center of the small room to consider. Floyd Trigg could be innocent, be guilty only of failure to know what was happening on his own ranch. It was possible. Many spreads were so large that owners never visited the more remote sections, particularly if the area was one of no value.

Dave's glance halted on a low, iron-bound chest in one corner of the room. A hasp and padlock secured its lid. He frowned. What could be so valuable in a blacksmith shop that it required lock and key?

He wasted no time in speculation. Picking up a short crowbar, he inserted the wedge under the hasp and threw his weight upon the shaft. Lock and all popped off with a sharp *crack.* Looking first to the yard and assuring himself he had attracted no attention, he leaned the crowbar against the wall and threw back the lid of the chest. A grunt of satisfaction escaped him. The box contained a dozen or more branding irons. His hunch had been right. Floyd Trigg was the one—the boss.

Taking up the iron on top, he examined it closely. The 66 brand. He tried to recall the mark, and then it came to him. Hyatt's brand was the Double D. By superimposing this iron upon a DD, it became a 66. He laid that one aside, took up another. An arrow. Pool's brand was a Tumbling A. Easily converted. There were several running irons in the chest—various curves and bars used for simple altering. One large iron bore the initials XED. He puzzled over that briefly, then recalled Eric Darrow's mark—an E-Bar-D. With the addition of a preceding X, the lines to change a single bar to an E, the result was a neat XED.

Saul Gans's brand, a solitary S, was the easiest of all to alter, and became a Circle 8. This probably accounted for the fact that Gans's herd was preyed upon continually by the rustlers who, supposedly working for him, drove off small jags of cattle at will.

Dave rose slowly. Now that he knew Trigg was guilty, he was finding it hard to believe. The ranchers of Fire Valley and the people of Apache Wells would find it difficult, too. They'd not take just his word for it, that was certain. They would demand proof.

He reckoned his best bet was Harvey Drace and the posse—if he could get near enough to the lawman to speak without being shot. And managing that, there still would be the task of convincing Drace, persuading him to return to the Circle 8 and have his look at the irons. But would there be time?

Dave shook his head worriedly. Veetch was due to take the branding irons to the men waiting in the brake. When he came for them, found the chest had been opened, he'd suspect. . . .

"What the hell you doing here?"

Dave froze at the harsh question, and then turned slowly. Floyd Trigg, pistol in hand, was standing in the doorway of the shed. The rancher's eyes flared with surprise as Ruskin faced him.

"You!" he blurted. "How did . . . ?"

Dave hurled himself at the man, dodging to one side to avoid the pistol. The weapon roared, filling the small shop with a deafening echo and hanging a pall of smoke in the air.

Ruskin felt the bullet tear at his collar, and then he collided with Trigg and the two of them went down. He struck at the rancher's face with his right hand, locked the left around the pistol. Trigg heaved him off, tried to regain his feet. Dave clung to the weapon, slugged at Trigg's jaw, felt pain shoot up his arm as his knuckles connected with the rancher's skull.

Trigg hesitated. Ruskin drove another blow to the man's head, felt him wilt slightly. Out in the yard someone was yelling. The gunshot had attracted the others.

Desperate, he slashed at Trigg's face with the heel of his hand, caught him across the bridge of the nose. The rancher gasped, fell back, fingers loosening their grip on the pistol. Ruskin wrenched it free, swung it at the man's head. The blow went true. The rancher groaned, went slack.

Instantly Ruskin pivoted, looked at the shadows moving into the doorway—Jess Veetch and Cully Moss. Behind them more of the Circle 8 crew were running up.

"He's mine!" Cully shouted, sweeping Veetch aside and drawing his pistol.

Dave shot him before his weapon had cleared leather. Veetch fired almost before he could swing around. Dave felt the bullet rip into his leg, was falling when he triggered his own pistol. Veetch jolted, began to stumble forward, muscle reflex firing his gun for the second time. Abruptly he collapsed.

On hands and knees Dave Ruskin stared toward the doorway, tried to see through the thick smoke. He could see vague shadows moving about—several. He had only two, perhaps three, bullets left.

"You in there . . . Ruskin?"

Dave sank to the ground. It was Harvey Drace. He lay for a long moment, and then rolled over and sat up.

"Come on in, Marshal!" he called. "Shooting's all done."

XX

The lawman, pistol drawn, stepped into the doorway, his bulk blocking the pale light now spreading across the land. Eric Darrow and two other men were at his heels.

"Good thing we decided to drop by Trigg's to mooch some breakfast offen his cook," a voice said from the outside. "Else we might've never found him.

Drace, weapon leveled at Ruskin, glanced around, said: "What's been going on here?"

"There's your rustlers," Dave said, pulling himself upright with considerable effort. "Leastwise, they're at the head of the gang. You'll find the others over in the brakes, camping in a box cañon. Couple hundred steers there, too . . . mostly mine."

The marshal's frown deepened. "You trying to tell me Floyd Trigg . . . ?"

"Take a look in that box there," Ruskin said, pointing at the chest. "You'll find all the proof you want. Probably more in the house . . . fake bills of sale and such from ranches that don't even exist."

Drace and Eric Darrow crowded forward, began to paw through the assortment of irons. The lawman was the first to turn away.

"I'm damned," he muttered. "Never figured it could be Floyd."

Ruskin nodded coldly. "You just decided it was Gans and let it go at that. You and all the rest of the ranchers around here."

"We were wrong," Darrow said, moving back into the center

of the room. "I'll say it now, but we had reason to feel that way . . . with Veetch and his bunch working out there." He paused, looked down at the man. "He dead, too?"

Drace knelt beside Veetch, rolled him to his back. "Won't be long . . . but we still got Trigg and the rest." Rising, he beckoned to Tobin, standing in the doorway. "Round up Floyd's crew, stash them in the bunkhouse, and put a guard over them. Then take some men, ride out to the brakes, and grab the others. I'll be waiting here."

The deputy wheeled away.

Trigg was struggling to sit up. The lawman faced him. "Floyd, I'm arresting you for the rustling that's been going on around here . . . got you cold. And I'm charging you with the killing of Rufe Hyatt, too."

The rancher rubbed at his jaw, focused his eyes on the lawman. "Didn't quite hear. . . ."

Drace repeated his words.

Trigg glanced around hurriedly, eyes suddenly bright. "Now . . . wait a minute, Harvey! I never killed Rufe . . . was that fool, Cully Moss."

"Cully's dead."

The rancher's frantic gaze halted on Veetch. "Ask him . . . he'll tell you!" Reaching out, he shook the dying man roughly. "Tell him, Jess! Tell him . . . damn you!"

Veetch groaned.

Drace leaned over him. "That the truth? Was it Cully who shot Hyatt, scratched Ruskin's name in the dirt?"

Veetch nodded wearily. The lawman stepped back, looked at Floyd Trigg. "Can't see as it makes much of a difference. Price you'll be paying is the same." He motioned at several of the posse members. "Put him in the bunkhouse with the others."

Dave, the wound in his leg throbbing fiercely, faced Harvey Drace. "You satisfied?"

"I am," the marshal said immediately. "Owe you an apology. Like Eric, I'm making it now."

Ruskin started for the door, halted beside Veetch. He studied the man's slack features for a moment, then said: "That five thousand dollars of Saul's . . . you get it?"

Veetch stirred. "Not five thousand . . . only a couple. Spent it . . . gone."

Dave waited for no more, continued on. Darrow caught up with him as he stepped haltingly into the morning light, and offered a supporting arm.

"That herd of yours in the brakes . . . I'll send some of my crew over, cut them out, drive them back to your place."

Dave shook his head. "Leave them be. Taking them into Dalhart."

"Won't leave you much to start ranching with."

"Can't be helped. Got to raise cash."

"Bank in town for that."

Ruskin shrugged. "Talked with Powell. He's not interested in making me a loan."

"He will be now," Darrow said. "Leave it to me."

Dave stared at the rancher. He should feel far from kindly toward him and the others of Fire Valley, but somehow he was finding it hard to hold a grudge. It was easy to be wrong, to make mistakes. He'd made a few himself.

"Obliged to you," he murmured, the stiffness gone from his manner.

"It's us who're obliged," Darrow said. "I'm hoping we can be friends . . . and I reckon I'm saying that for everybody around here. They'll look at it same way as me."

"Glad of that. Figure on being around here for a long time. Now, I'd like to get this leg fixed up a bit, then there's a little errand I need to do before I head for home."

"Errand?"

"Got to drop by, thank a lady for lending me her horse . . . and standing by me."

Eric Darrow's mouth opened with surprise, and then he grinned. "She'll like that. If you don't mind, I'll ride along. Happens I'm going that way."

"Don't mind at all," Ruskin said.

ABOUT THE AUTHOR

Ray Hogan was an author who inspired a loyal following over the years since he published his first Western novel, *Ex-Marshal,* in 1956. Hogan was born in Willow Springs, Missouri. At five the Hogan family moved to Albuquerque where they lived in the foothills of the Sandia and Manzano Mountains. From the beginning he did exhaustive research into the history and the people of the Old West. Above all, what is most impressive about Hogan's Western novels is the consistent quality with which each is crafted, the compelling depth of his characters, and his ability to juxtapose the complexities of human conflict into narratives as interesting as emotionally involving. *Panhandle Gunman* will be his next Five Star Western.